I was staring off into space when a wisp of smoke caught my eye. It was weird smoke—blue and sparkly, as if someone had sprinkled it with glitter. And it was seeping in through the window.

"What the—" I hit a sharp chord and sprang off the piano bench. What kind of fire would create blue smoke?

As I crept toward the window, the smoke whirled and changed shape. It formed a giant hand. Then it snaked through the air, reaching out, spreading its giant fingers...

And grabbed me around the waist!

Before I could scream, it began to squeeze me, sending a cold chill through my body.

I tugged at the blue fingers, trying to loosen the grip. Then I tried to twist and squirm. But every time I moved, the grip seemed to tighten.

"Let me go!" A hopeless feeling welled up inside me. I was going to be squeezed to death!

**Read these books in
the SHADOW ZONE series:**

The Ghost of Chicken Liver Hill
Guess Who's Dating a Werewolf?
The Witches Next Door

**And zapping your way from
the SHADOW ZONE soon:**

Revenge of the Computer Phantoms
The Undead Express
Good Night, Mummy!

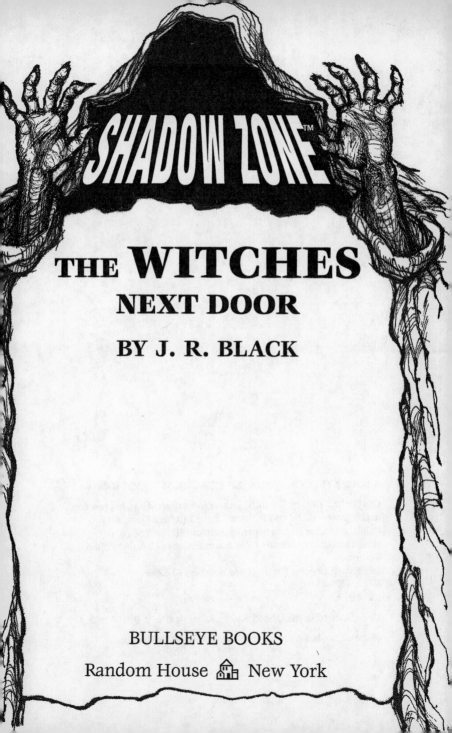

SHADOW ZONE™

THE WITCHES
NEXT DOOR

BY J. R. BLACK

BULLSEYE BOOKS

Random House 🏠 New York

A BULLSEYE BOOK PUBLISHED BY RANDOM HOUSE, INC.

Library of Congress Catalog Card Number: 93-83968
ISBN: 0-679-85108-9
RL: 4.9

Manufactured in the United States of America   10 9 8 7 6 5 4 3 2 1

SHADOW ZONE is a trademark of Twelfth House Productions.

1

Hold Your Nose

Did you ever get a whiff of a moldy wet sneaker? How about a rotten egg? Well, the awful smell was a cross between sneakers and stinky eggs. And it was coming from the house next door.

"Not again," my mom said. She wrinkled her nose as she stepped out of the house, ready to drive me to my piano recital.

"Stink city," I said, looking over at our neighbors' rickety house. Wild rose vines climbed up two sides of it and what was left was hidden by fir trees. Other than the plants that were ready to swallow up the place, there was no sign of life.

"Well, hold your nose and get in the car," Mom said, crossing the driveway.

"Maybe the Nightingales are dead," I said. "Maybe their bodies are rotting inside the house." After all, we hadn't seen the two old ladies since the day they'd moved in a little over a month ago.

Mom frowned. "That's a terrible thing to say. Especially about two sweet old ladies."

Sweet? Not even the roses could cover up the smell that came from their house. Something really weird was going on over there.

I turned toward the car just as someone called from down the block.

"Elaine! Elaine, do you have a minute?" It was Mrs. Stephens, who lived on the corner. Since we'd come to Oregon six months ago, I had seen enough of Mrs. Stephens to know her type. Obnoxious. Just like her daughter Chelsea, who was in my grade at school.

"Hello, Maura." Mom walked away from the car with a forced smile. "Actually, we were just on our way to Jennifer's piano recital."

"This won't take a minute," Mrs. Stephens said. She pointed to the house next door. "That stench is getting out of control. Unless you can get your neighbors to stop it, I'm phoning the police this afternoon."

"The police..." Mom frowned. "Isn't that a little extreme?"

"Well, I can't live another day with that foul smell hanging in the air," Mrs. Stephens said.

2

"Who knows what causes it? Not to mention the health hazards. There must be someone I can call at the health department."

"The smell is certainly...unpleasant," Mom said carefully. "But we're talking about two elderly women. The sight of the police might give them a fright."

"We have to do *something* to stop the smell," Mrs. Stephens insisted.

"Why don't we go talk to them," Mom suggested.

Clear the air, I thought, hiding a snicker. I followed Mom up the overgrown walkway to the Nightingales' house. Since I'd been dreading the piano recital all week, I didn't mind the detour. Besides, I wanted to get a closer look at our neighbors.

Mrs. Stephens walked beside my mother, holding a monogrammed handkerchief over her nose.

Mom pressed the doorbell. No answer. She knocked at the door. The house was quiet and deserted. Where were they?

Mom knocked a bit harder while Mrs. Stephens marched across the lawn and around the corner of the house. I figured she was seeking the source of the smell, so I followed her.

And there, tucked into a row of shrubs, was an old shed. It looked harmless. But, boy, did it stink!

Mrs. Stephens coughed, then pinched her nose through the handkerchief. "This is where it's coming from." She rubbed the windowpane, trying to see inside. "What on earth are they doing in there?"

Curious, I stood on my toes for a look. After all, there had to be something really rotten to cause such a horrible smell. Maybe the Nightingales really were dead. But if they were, we certainly couldn't see the bodies through the window. It was completely misted up, like a mirror in the bathroom when you take a hot shower.

"They must have gone out," Mom called to us. I knew that was impossible. The Nightingale sisters never left the house. At least, not while I was awake. "We'll have to try again later. If you—"

Then it happened. The door of the shed flew open with a bang. My glasses slipped down my nose as I jumped clear of the door. Thick white mist poured out the doorway.

"Oooof!" Mrs. Stephens gasped in alarm.

"Oh, my. We *do* have visitors." The swirling mist gave way to a mishmash of ruffles, wrinkles, and silver hair.

4

Pushing my glasses into place, I focused on the Nightingale sisters. They were like two wrinkled apple dolls dressed in lavender gowns. One was tall, thin, and stately. The other was short and round like a snowman. Both of them wore round glasses.

"I *told* you I heard something, Emma," said the tall sister. She turned to us. "I'm so sorry to keep you waiting. But as you can see, we've been busy."

"Yes, I do see. And I can smell it, too," Mrs. Stephens said as my mother came around the corner of the house.

"Sorry to bother you, ladies," Mom said, "but, to be honest, some of the neighbors have been, um, concerned by the, uh, odors coming from your property."

"It stinks," snapped Mrs. Stephens.

"Oh, dear," said the round one with a sigh.

"Must be your new recipe, Emma," said the tall one.

"Must be," said Emma. "Oh, dear!" She sighed again, her finger sinking into her pudgy cheek.

"We'll just have to work on the scent," the tall one said. "Can't offend the neighbors."

"Of course not," Emma agreed. She nodded her head toward my mother and Mrs. Stephens. "Please accept our apologies. Abigail and I are just not the sniffers we once were. We could use a younger nose," she added, turning to me.

"Yes," Abigail agreed. "And a pair of young hands would help, too. We've had so much trouble settling in."

I stepped back and looked down at a clump of weeds. I wasn't about to let one of them catch my eye. Being lonely was one thing. But there was no way I was going to spend my time with two old ladies!

"Then you'll clean it up? Whatever *it* is that smells so disgusting?" Mrs. Stephens asked. She craned her neck, trying to see beyond the sisters into the shed.

I was doing the same thing, but I couldn't see past the wall of mist behind them. Then Abigail reached back and firmly shut the door.

"Of course!" Emma promised, her hands fluttering.

"Not to worry," said Abigail.

"Thanks for being so understanding," Mom said with a smile. She turned up the walk, and the two sisters floated along beside her, chattering away. Mrs. Stephens didn't seem totally satisfied, but she followed them anyway.

Left alone, I stared at the shed door. What kind of recipe could create such a terrible smell?

I mean, was it something they planned on *eating*?

I carefully pushed the door open, but I still couldn't see through the thick mist. Just then a breeze kicked up and the wall of smoke faded for a moment. In that second I saw a huge round object. Around it glowed a bright blue halo. It was a tub—a cauldron! And it was filled with something blue that bubbled and spat as it simmered. Then the mist closed in again.

I didn't know what the Nightingales were cooking. But I sure didn't want a taste.

"Jennifer..." called a voice from inside the shed. It sounded giddy, like a cartoon elf.

"Who's there?" I stepped forward into the mist. I gagged as the foul smell hit me.

"We've come for you," the voice said merrily.

Was this some sort of joke? "Who's in there?" I said sternly.

The voice began to laugh. I could hear the cauldron rumbling and spitting. Afraid of getting burned, or worse, by whatever the cauldron held, I backed away.

If this was some sort of game, I didn't want to play anymore.

I pulled the door shut and raced out to the street. But I couldn't escape the bone-chilling sound of laughter.

2

Toil and Trouble

The weird voice haunted me even after Mom and I met Dad at the town hall for my piano recital.

When it was my turn to play, I couldn't stop thinking of the spitting cauldron in the shed.

My hands trembled over the ivory keys, and I heard it again. *"Jennifer...we've come for you."*

My brain stalled. My fingers froze. My heart raced. Normally, I would have swallowed my fear and banged through the piece. But this was no ordinary stage fright. It was as if I'd been hypnotized.

The voice came again. *"Play!"* it demanded. Then it giggled.

Who said that? I looked out into the audience. But the faces that stared back at me were blank and bored. Couldn't anyone else hear it?

Suddenly, my hands came down on the piano keys and I was playing. But my fingers had a life of their own! They wiggled and stretched like rubber-legged dancers. Amazed, I watched my hands work the keys like a pro!

Whoa. What was happening to me? Had some strange power taken over my body? Was I...was I *possessed*?

In a flash, it was over. The audience clapped. I slid off the bench. Dazed, I took a deep breath, bowed, and walked off the stage.

By the time I joined my parents in the audience, I felt better. My hands still tingled, but at least I seemed to have control over them again. As for the voice, it must have been a severe case of recital jitters. At least that's what I told myself.

All the way home in the car, Mom and Dad talked about my performance. This, of course, led Mom into thinking about different kinds of lessons I should take. She thought it would be a good idea for me to start playing the violin. As if an afternoon of violin lessons could make up for the fact that I hadn't made any friends since we'd moved here.

"Bob Calavicci told me his son has been asked to join Junior Symphony," Dad said. "I bet you'll be next." He turned to the back seat to give me a thumbs-up sign.

The last thing I needed was to be lumped in

with kids like Todd Calavicci. Cow-lah-VEE-chee. Even his name was weird. "Todd Calavicci is a nerd," I said.

"It's not nice to talk that way about your friends," Mom said.

"He's not my friend."

"Well, maybe he should be," Mom replied, which, of course, made me feel awful.

I pushed my glasses into place and sank into the back seat. It wasn't my fault that I hadn't made any friends since we'd moved. Most of the girls in my class had been together since grade school, and they were pretty tight. Girls like Chelsea Stephens and Kristy Geist didn't need to make friends with shy girls who didn't have a lot to say. Girls like me.

Don't get me wrong. I had lots of friends back in Ohio, where we used to live. Things just hadn't clicked for me here. At least, not yet. Mom had promised to let my best friend Megan come visit me this summer for a month. Even though we wrote letters, I missed Megan a lot. In the meantime, I was stuck here, the new kid at Lake Trawley Middle School.

The car stopped at a light, and I noticed a group of kids walking to the shopping center. They were probably going to Electric Mania, the video arcade. It was right next to a burger place called Here's the Beef. Everyone hung out there. Everyone except me.

I decided to write Megan a letter as soon as we got home. I'd tell her all about the cauldron and the bad smell next door. But for now, I wouldn't mention the weird voice or the way my fingers had gone crazy at the recital. Some things are just too hard to explain in a letter.

Double, double, toil and trouble.
Fire burn and cauldron bubble!

I closed my eyes and shuddered at the image of cackling witches dancing around a cauldron. Did Mr. Suarez have to pick *this week* to make us read about witches? Shakespeare sure pulled out all the stops when he wrote *Macbeth*.

Witches. The thought of that blue, steaming cauldron had kept me up half the night. I couldn't stop worrying about what the Nightingale sisters were up to. But I knew that there was no such thing as a witch. Besides, witches didn't wear purple ruffles and spectacles, did they?

I propped my notebook on my lap and reached for my knapsack. Like the rest of the kids who'd stayed after school, I was sitting in the auditorium, trying to finish my homework. We were waiting for a meeting about the annual lip-synch contest to begin. Mrs. Wertz, otherwise known as Mrs. Worst, was going to explain the rules.

"Are you trying out?" asked a voice behind me.

It was Todd Calavicci.

"I, um, don't know," I said. *Good one, Jen.* I couldn't even muster up the courage to talk to a nerd who lived three doors away from me.

Todd sank into the seat beside me. Oh, great. Now he would want to talk.

You might wonder what I was doing at the meeting if I wasn't going to be in the contest. The truth was, I wanted to be in a lip-synch act. But I didn't have the nerve to burst into Lake Trawley Middle School's "event" of the year. Get up in front of the student body and all their parents to perform? Forget it!

I sneaked a glance at Todd. Freckles covered his nose. His dark brown hair was a little long. It curled over his collar and on his forehead. He looked pretty normal, like those kids you see in ads for breakfast cereal. His nerdism came from the things he did, not the way he looked.

"I heard that you're trying out for Junior Symphony," Todd said.

"More like my parents are forcing me to."

He shrugged. "I didn't want to be in it at

first, but it's not that bad."

I gave him a cold look, hoping he'd get the message and scram. He didn't budge.

A squeal sounded from the row in front of me. Chelsea Stephens wagged her finger at one of the boys in her group. "You're soooo bad!" she cooed. He grinned, eating up the attention.

Chelsea always made a big scene. I turned back to my homework and tried to read the witches' chant again.

Fire burn and cauldron bubble.

"Reading about the witches, huh?" Todd asked.

I nodded.

"I had Mr. Suarez last year," Todd said. "He's okay."

I glanced at Todd. He just wasn't going to go away. If I had to sit next to a nerd, I might as well squeeze some information out of him.

"What do you know about the Nightingale sisters?" I asked.

"Your neighbors?" He grinned. "I've gotten a whiff of their house. Why does it stink so much?"

"You know that shed behind it?" He nodded. "Well," I said, "they've got a cauldron in there. They're cooking something gross.

Something that bubbles and stinks."

"Really?" Todd seemed impressed.

Suddenly Chelsea spun around. Her brown eyes zeroed in on me.

"Oooh, does it really bubble?" she asked, opening her eyes wide and putting her hands on her cheeks in mock horror. Her friends snickered.

I shrank down in my seat, wishing I were invisible.

"A cauldron," Chelsea said. She tucked her long wavy red hair behind her ears, glancing to see who was watching. "No wonder their house stinks. Did they try to push you in?" she added, raising her voice. "I always knew those ladies were weird. But I didn't know they were *witches!*"

"Better watch out," Bryan O'Donnell said, pointing at me, "or they'll chase you on their broomsticks."

That got a round of laughter from everyone. My face got hot, and I hoped no one would notice that it was turning red.

Just then Kristy Geist came up the aisle and nudged her friend. Kristy was Chelsea's counterpart—pretty and popular, except that she had black hair. "C'mon, Chelsea," she said. "Mrs. Worst wants all the contestants on stage."

"All right. I'm going to wrap this contest up," Chelsea boasted. She looked at me and snickered. "Unless Jennifer casts a spell on me."

"You don't have to worry, Chelsea," Todd said. "Witches don't go after girls who are stuck on themselves. Gives them indigestion."

Chelsea sucked in her breath, shocked that anyone had the nerve to stand up to her. I was surprised, too. The guy actually had guts.

"I got a great idea," Bryan said. "Let's spy on the witches. Maybe their house is haunted."

"Yeah," the rest of the kids chorused.

"Let's do it," Chelsea agreed. "We'll meet at seven o'clock tonight. In front of the old ladies' house. It should be dark."

"Wait a minute..." I said, trying to stop them. But it was too late. Chelsea and her friends were scrambling onto the stage.

What had I done?

It was a cool spring night. The sky was as clear as glass, and the air smelled of roses. At last, the Nightingales had gotten that awful smell out of their "recipe." But I had a bad feeling about tonight. I was just as curious about my neighbors as any kid on the block, but I didn't trust Chelsea. What was she planning?

As I pushed my glasses into place, I spotted

15

the cluster of kids at the end of the street. Chelsea led the pack, followed by Kristy, Bryan, and a bunch of other kids. Todd was there, too, which made me feel better. At least he had sense. Maybe it was going to be okay.

Then I heard Todd ask, "What are you going to do with those eggs?"

My stomach sank as I noticed the egg cartons that Chelsea and Bryan held. The group marched to the edge of the Nightingales' lawn, then stopped.

"Now, wait a minute—" I began.

But before I could say another word, Bryan threw back his head and called out, "Come out, come out, wherever you are!"

The other kids joined in, chanting and laughing.

Flickering lights came on inside the Nightingales' house. My heart pounded.

"I don't think we should do this," Kristy said. She frowned at the house, then shoved her hands into her jeans pockets.

"Kristy's right," I said. "They're just nice old ladies. The cauldron thing was a joke."

Chelsea wrinkled her nose. "I don't care. That smell was no joke. They shouldn't be allowed to get away with something like that."

The door opened. The Nightingales floated

outside, holding up candles.

"Who's there?" Abigail called. Her voice sounded thin and weak.

"The witches!" Bryan screamed.

Chelsea opened the carton and pulled out an egg. "Let's get 'em—before they get us!" she shouted, then hurled an egg at the house.

"Bombs away!" Bryan tore open his own carton and pelted the Nightingales' porch.

Abigail and Emma stood still as statues while eggs smashed around them.

"We missed!" Chelsea cried.

"Hags!" Bryan glanced at Chelsea for approval. She nodded and he grabbed another egg. But before Bryan could toss it, something smashed onto the ground at his feet. Then another egg splattered against Chelsea's shoe.

"Eeew!" she cried. "Gross!"

I looked up in amazement. Eggs were flying back at us!

But no one was throwing them!

3

Feeling Mousy

Like a mean curve ball, an egg came spinning toward me. I ducked, just in time.

Bryan wasn't so lucky. One hit him right in the forehead. He groaned and swiped at the splattered mess.

"Run!" Chelsea yelled.

The group scattered, scrambling to get away from the shower of eggs. Bryan dived behind a hedge, and I saw an egg follow, as if it had a homing device. I'd never seen anything like it.

In a moment, only Todd and I were left standing in front of the Nightingales' house. One last egg whizzed by my ear, and then the attack ended. Through the light of dusk, I could see Emma and Abigail standing on their porch. They peered at us, then floated back inside.

A painful silence hung in the air. I swallowed and said, "I feel awful. This whole thing was my fault."

"Did you see that egg hit Bryan?" Todd asked, as if he couldn't believe what he'd seen.

I nodded. "It was weird."

"*Really* weird," he said. "Do you think the old ladies are angry?"

"Who knows? But one thing's for sure. No one deserves to be attacked like that." I turned toward the walkway. "Maybe I should apologize."

"Now?" Todd said. "What about the eggs? I mean, you could get pelted again."

"I'll take my chances." I didn't want to go, but something seemed to be moving my legs. Like the force that made my fingers dance on the piano, it pushed me forward. I was walking forward, faster and faster. I could hear Todd's voice, but I couldn't turn back to answer him. On the Nightingales' front porch I skidded to a halt.

What was happening to me? This time, I was having trouble passing it off as my imagination. *My body was taking on a life of its own!* My mouth formed a silent scream as the door yawned open.

Emma and Abigail stood in the doorway. A mixing bowl was cradled in Emma's arm. She was beating its contents with a wire whisk.

They looked perfectly normal. Were these the same women who'd mixed up the smelly brew in a cauldron? The neighbors whose shed possessed a voice that laughed at me and called me by name?

Abigail eyed me seriously. "I sense a problem."

"I'm sorry," I choked. "I didn't mean for this to happen. Some kids at school heard me talking about you."

Just then Emma tipped the bowl and batter spilled over the side. Before I could react, a few drops of multicolored liquid fell onto my arm.

"Oh, Emma! Clumsy you!" Abigail scolded.

"So sorry, dear," Emma said.

Just a few drops had hit me. But they sank into my skin, making me shiver.

One moment I was as tall as they were. The next, I felt as if I'd melted to the ground, my nose at their hemlines!

I squinted up at the towering sisters. Way up there, I could see their faces. I tried to speak, but all I could manage was a faint squeak.

A squeak? What was going on? I felt as small as a field mouse!

Somewhere above me a bird squawked. Fear rippled through me. A bird of prey...if I wasn't careful, I'd end up as dinner!

"Better undo the damage," Abigail said, her voice echoing from above.

Splat! Something hit my head. It felt like a heavy raindrop from the sky.

Then, quick as a sneeze, it was over. I felt normal again, and tall enough to see the ruffled lace around Emma's neck.

"Wh-what happened?" I asked.

"Oh, nothing, dear," Emma explained. "Are you okay? You didn't look quite like yourself for a moment."

I didn't feel like myself either, I thought.

"I think we licked that dreadful odor problem." Abigail's thin face broke into a smile as she changed the subject. "But don't you worry. And never mind about those rascals outside. Emma and I were young once, too. We know what mischief children can get into."

Emma's silver head bobbed. "Oh, my, yes! Every class has one bad apple. In our schooldays, there was that dreadful Willie Witherspoon."

"A wicked boy if I ever saw one." Abigail clucked her tongue. "Almost as bad as Chelsea Stephens. Doesn't she remind you of a snake?"

I was surprised. "You know Chelsea?"

"We can spot troublemakers from miles away. By the way, dear, they always get what's coming to them," Emma said. "Always."

"Always," Abigail agreed. Her voice was suddenly icy.

Then, just as suddenly, it was warm again as she asked, "Now that we've settled that mess, won't you join us for tea?"

I shook my head. It felt as if it were stuffed with cotton. "I—I've got to get home. I feel kind of funny. I mean, what is that stuff you're mixing? What did you just do to me?"

"If you're feeling odd, don't think about it. I'm sure it will pass," Abigail advised.

"Nonsense," Emma objected. "The truth is, well—you were a mouse, dear. But just for a moment. And you were feeling pretty mousy *before* the potion touched you, weren't you?"

I stared at her. I was having a hard time believing this. "Let's keep this as our little secret," Emma went on. She winked at me. "One witch to another."

Witch! Was it possible that they really *were* witches? But if they were, they had me all wrong. I was just a normal girl—and a chicken-hearted normal girl at that.

"W-wait," I stammered. "This can't be happening. There's no such thing as witches, so you *can't be* witches. And I'm certainly not a witch."

"Well, you'd better accept that we are indeed witches. As for you, you're not a witch yet, dear," Emma said sweetly. "But that's why we've come for you."

"The truth of the matter is, we've been looking all over the world for you, Jennifer," Abigail said. "We've come to Lake Trawley to make you a witch. It was supposed to be a wonderful surprise!"

"Wonderful?" I croaked.

4

Bat Attack!

I stared at my neighbors in horror. Why in the world would a kid like me want to grow warts, wear a black hat, and cackle over a cauldron of smelly brew?

"No, thanks," I said firmly. Inside my head I was thinking that I must be going nuts to take this all seriously.

"But you're going to love it!" Emma exclaimed.

"The job does have its perks," Abigail said. "But you have to be patient."

"Oh, yes!" Emma nodded her head. "Training takes time."

"And we mustn't make a mistake," Abigail warned.

"That would be disastrous!" Emma agreed.

I looked from one old lady to the other. They were serious. Seriously crazy. And if I didn't get out of there fast, they'd use me for stew meat in that big old cauldron.

"My mom's going to be wondering where I am," I said, backing away slowly.

"Then we'll see you tomorrow, dear," Emma said, adjusting the mixing bowl in her arm.

"Tomorrow?" I shook my head. "No. I have school. And lessons. And—"

"Tomorrow it is," Abigail said as if I had never spoken. She nodded once, then shut the door.

I pressed my glasses onto my nose and raced into the dark night. Through the weeds. Into the street. Into our driveway. Home at last.

But even after I'd climbed into bed and pulled the covers over my head, I still didn't feel safe. And I couldn't stop from shaking when I heard the giddy voice echo through my room. *Jennifer...we've come for you!*

The next day, the Lark Street egg war was the talk of the school. Todd spread the word about how I'd faced the witches after the battle. I'm not sure if anyone believed him, or even cared. On the other hand, Chelsea was mad that her favorite high-top sneakers had gotten egged. And she blamed me.

"*Someone* must have tipped those hags off,"

she said. She glared as I shoved my books into my locker. "Someone like their wimpy next-door neighbor."

"I didn't tell them you were coming," I said. "I didn't even *know* you were planning to egg their house. That was mean and rotten."

Chelsea rolled her eyes, as if I were a hopeless loser. "What's rotten is your sense of humor. And you'd better hope that I don't get into trouble over this. Because I don't get mad. I get even."

After school there was even more music to face—and I don't mean my piano lesson. Somehow, my mother had heard about the egg throwing. And she was steaming mad.

"What were you thinking?" she asked me. "Vandalizing a neighbor's home! Jen, how *could* you?"

What could I say? That I'd been hearing voices? That I'd found a cauldron full of brew? That our neighbors wanted to make me a witch?

It was no use trying to defend myself. As punishment I was sent over to help the Nightingales with chores after my piano lesson. My own mother had promised me as a servant to two sworn witches. Sometimes life just isn't fair.

"Have you come to start your training?" Emma

asked when I'd dragged myself over to their house.

"No," I said glumly. "I don't want to be a witch."

"Oh, dear," Emma said. "Where's your sense of fun, Jennifer?"

That sounded familiar.

"It will come in time," Abigail said. "How about some tea, then?"

I shook my head. "My mother says you have some chores for me."

"You'll need a more positive attitude," Abigail said.

"Oh, yes!" Emma agreed, nodding furiously. "Much, much more!"

"We'll start with tea, then we'll see what needs to be done," Abigail said.

Before I could get up the energy to run home, I was ushered into their living room.

"Just wait here," Abigail ordered. "We'll be right back." They glided off to the rear of the house.

I looked around, shaking my head. It was straight out of another century! The chairs had curved wooden legs and purple velvet seats. The lamps were covered with satin shades and fringe. I touched one and realized it was filled with oil. No electric lights for the Nightingales. Oh, no. That would be too normal.

The carpet was patterned with huge roses in pink and gray and black. In the center of the room was a round marble table. A huge leather book lay open on it. Across both pages was a drawing of a hideous green snake.

BLACK MAMBA was written below the picture in fancy script. Underneath, in smaller script, it said, "This poisonous African snake is green when it is young, and becomes dark brown as it matures. Its bite is often fatal."

I shivered and slammed the book shut. A puff of dust filled the air, and I moved away.

There was a stuffed owl on the mantel. I stared into its orange eyes as clocks began to chime. Next to the owl was a gold cuckoo clock. Five o'clock. It was time to scram.

A weird feeling swept over me. I whipped around, sure that I was being watched. The owl's eyes had blinked. *Blinked!* Or had they?

"I have to get out of here," I whispered.

Screech!

I nearly jumped out of my skin at the sudden shriek and loud flapping sound. I was about to bolt when I noticed the cloth-covered cage behind me. I lifted the cloth, and the bird squawked again.

"Hey, don't worry. I'm not planning on staying long," I assured him. He had fat, wrinkled claws and rumpled white feathers. Kind of a mangy thing.

The bird let out another ear-splitting screech when Emma and Abigail appeared in the doorway.

"Harold," Abigail said with a frown.

Emma sighed. "That vile creature. He has a terrible disposition. Always had."

I nodded, wondering why they kept a pet that was so cranky. "Does he talk?" I asked, wondering about the voice I'd been hearing.

"Yes," Emma answered, "but don't get him started. Harold never has a kind word to say."

"Oh, well. Here we are," Abigail said, smiling brightly. She moved the book and put a silver tea set on the table. She poured three cups of tea and my heart sank as I realized they expected me to drink some. I'd never liked tea. And I didn't trust these two with anything that resembled cooking.

"Thanks," I said, taking the cup. While they sipped, I pretended to drink. Luckily, they didn't seem to notice that no tea passed my lips.

"The roses by the walkway are awfully leggy," Abigail said. "They're begging for a clipping."

"They need to be cut," said Emma. She

moved her fingers like a pair of scissors. "Chop, chop!"

I swallowed hard. Her blue eyes looked cold and evil.

"But I can't prune like I used to," she went on. "Would you mind helping out, Jennifer?"

"We'd pay you, of course," Abigail added.

"Uh, sure," I said. I tried not to look at the clock. How much longer before I could do the chores and sneak away?

"And the basement!" Abigail clucked.

"Those boxes need to be stacked against the wall," said Emma.

"Before someone gets hurt," Abigail added.

"I'll move them," I said.

Emma clapped her hands together in delight. "Would you, dear?"

"Wonderful." Abigail set down her cup with a thump. "Let's start right now." She took my cup and led me toward the back of the house past the kitchen.

"Now to the task at hand," Abigail said, opening the basement door. "It's those boxes at the bottom." She pointed. Through the darkness I could barely make out a stack of boxes at the bottom of the wooden steps.

I looked around for the light switch. Then I remembered. No electricity! I swallowed hard against the musty smell. Did I really have to go down there by myself?

"Be careful," Emma advised as I stepped down.

I gripped the rail. It felt sturdier than it looked. While the Nightingales waited at the top of the stairs, I went down into the cobwebby darkness.

What horrors awaited me in this pit? Worms and spiders? Rattling bones? Moaning ghosts? With the Nightingales I'd learned to expect the worst.

By the time I reached the cement floor, I had completely creeped myself out with gory visions. Just finish the job and leave! I told myself. I lifted the first box, which wasn't too heavy.

"Stack them on the wooden shelves," Abigail called down. "The ones against the wall."

I shoved the box onto the shelf and looked over my shoulder. I could hear the Nightingales whispering at the top of the stairs. A few fading beams of sunlight slanted through the cracks in a boarded-up window. Torn cobwebs hung from the ceiling, and dust motes swirled through the air. It was spooky, but in the same way that a lot of old basements were.

I was relieved in a way, but still eager to finish and flee. So I started stacking. The job was easier than I'd expected. My imagination had nearly gotten the best of me.

Then I heard a flapping noise. Something moved in the air over my head. I looked up. It was something furry. I froze. The hairs on my arms lifted.

What was down here?

Whoosh! Whatever it was had flown past my face, fluttering and squeaking.

I squinted into the darkness trying to see my attacker. Then all of a sudden it was right in front of me.

A bat! And it was heading my way!

5

Where There's Smoke...

I screamed. The bat squeaked in my ear. Then its wings smacked through the air as it circled over me.

I dropped the box and hunched down.

"Don't be sad. Don't be blue! The Nightingales are fond of you!"

That voice! I recognized the giddy sound.

"Who said that?" I croaked, looking up. But when I lowered my arms, the bat dived at my face. Its wings flapped, and I felt its claws tangling in my hair.

"Stop it!" I yelled, ducking away. I covered my face and stumbled back against the cement wall. Then the bat disappeared into the shadows behind the furnace.

"A talking bat?" I muttered.

"No sense of fun!" I heard a giggle. But it wasn't coming from the bat. It was coming out of thin air!

"Are you all right, dear?" Abigail called down.

I stood up and ran my fingers through my hair. "I'm okay," I called back, trying to calm myself so that my hands would stop shaking.

In eerie silence, I stowed the last two boxes, then bolted up the stairs.

"Oh, dear." Emma's eyes popped open when I burst into the kitchen. "Something wrong?"

"There's a bat down there," I said.

"A visitor?" Abigail smiled. "Must have gotten in through the heating vent."

"Oh, think of it! In our very own basement," Emma said, clapping her hands in joy.

"It flew into my hair," I said, looking for a little sympathy.

"Did it really?" Emma smiled at me as if I were the luckiest girl in the world. "Lovely!"

I pushed my glasses up on my nose and glared at the witches. You'd think I'd just discovered a movie star in their basement.

"Oh, dear." Emma frowned, blinking at me. "Don't worry. Bats are harmless creatures, you know. Don't look so unhappy." She turned to Abigail. "Poor thing, she's tired."

"Very tired," Abigail agreed. "You can prune the roses some other day." Leading me to the door, she pressed several crumpled bills into my palm. "You passed the test," she whispered as I opened the door.

I wasn't sure what she meant. But I didn't want to stick around to find out.

That night after dinner, I sat at the piano absent-mindedly practicing scales. My parents were at the movies, and I was feeling sorry for myself. I thought about Megan and my old friends. Back in Ohio, there were no witches or nasty girls like Chelsea. At least, not that I could remember.

I was staring off into space when a wisp of smoke caught my eye. It was weird smoke—blue and sparkly, as if someone had sprinkled it with glitter. And it was seeping in through the window.

"What the—" I hit a sharp chord and sprang off the piano bench. What kind of fire would create blue smoke?

As I crept toward the window, the smoke whirled and changed shape. It formed a giant hand. Then it snaked through the air, reaching out, spreading its giant fingers...

And grabbed me around the waist!

Before I could scream, it began to squeeze me, sending a cold chill through my body.

I tugged at the blue fingers, trying to loosen the grip. Then I tried to twist and squirm.

But every time I moved, the grip seemed to tighten.

"Let me go!" A hopeless feeling welled up inside me. I was going to be squeezed to death!

My arms felt numb, as if they didn't belong to me anymore. Then they began to tremble. I watched as they pushed down to the bottom of the big blue hand.

It's happening again, I thought. What's worse, being squeezed to death by a giant smoke hand or being possessed?

It wasn't a question I could answer.

I saw my fingers dig into the edge of the smoke. Suddenly, I felt a surge of power through my arms. Before I could even think about it, I hoisted the giant fist over my head and tossed it off, like a sweater that was too small.

The smoke shriveled into a ball. Then it bounced across the floor and hopped out the window.

I pressed my nose to the glass. Outside tendrils of smoke shrank away from my house. As the air cleared, I could see the Nightingales' house. And—big surprise—blue smoke swirled around it.

Was the smoky fist just another one of their "accidents"? Or had they sent it on purpose?

Suddenly a black figure ran across the lawn. It was Todd Calavicci. "Fire!" he shouted. "Somebody help!"

He was trying to rescue the witches! Some hero. If he didn't watch it, they'd squeeze the life out of him, too.

I ran out of the house and raced into the yard next door.

"Stay back," I warned Todd. I grabbed his arm and tried to stop him, but he was stronger than I was. He edged across the Nightingales' lawn, dragging me with him.

"They have to get out!" He tried to shake me off. "They'll be burned to a crisp."

"It's not a normal fire," I told him. "The smoke has no smell, but it's dangerous. You'd better stay away."

Before my eyes the smoke changed from blue to red to green. It shimmered and twisted and rose into the shape of a skull. Then it became a swarm of bats. I ducked fast.

"We've got to save them," Todd said. He stuck his foot into the wall of smoke, testing it. Like a running stream, it swirled around his toe. "I don't like the looks of this."

"Me neither!" I tugged on his arm, but he pulled away.

"Come on," Todd said. Before I could stop him, he plunged into the smoke and disappeared.

"Todd!" I called. Why wouldn't he listen to me?

I had no choice but to go after him. I took a deep breath, then stepped into the smoke. Blinded, I felt my way up the porch steps and through the open front door.

Inside the vestibule, the air was clear. There was no smoke in the house! In fact, it looked perfectly normal.

Todd blinked in surprise. "Where's the fire?"

"I told you it wasn't a normal fire," I said. "Let's get out of here while—"

"Is that you, Jennifer?" Emma's round face appeared in the kitchen doorway. "Oh! Pardon me. Who are you, young man?"

Snagged! I felt myself blush, but I tried my best to act normal.

"This is Todd Calavicci," I said. "We saw smoke. Todd thought there was a fire."

"Oh, no, no, no. Just a little mistake, that's all," Abigail said, floating out beside her sister. "So this is Mr. Calavicci." She looked him up and down. "We've been expecting you."

"You have?" Todd asked.

"Of course. It's our business to know what's

important to Jennifer."

"Todd isn't—" I was about to blurt out "important," but then thought better of it.

Harold screeched as we walked into the living room. It sounded as if he were trying to spit out some words. Abigail scolded him until he shut up.

"Mind if we look around?" Todd asked.

Emma's eyes narrowed on Todd. I held my breath, half-expecting her to turn him to dust or something. "No need to bother, Mr. Calavicci. As you can see, there is no fire."

"Where'd that smoke come from?" Todd asked.

"Just an experiment." Abigail waved off the matter. "Nothing important. Unless, of course, the smell bothered you. It wasn't bad, was it?"

"Our olfactory senses aren't so good anymore," Emma explained.

"The smoke didn't smell," I said, adjusting my glasses. "But it had a mind of its own. It formed weird shapes. Like a skull. And a fist that could squeeze the life out of you."

Abigail clucked. "How frightening," she said sympathetically. But the look in her eyes chilled me to the bone. She lapped up my fear like a thirsty cat!

"Oh, dear." Emma stuck a finger into her dimpled face. "The recipe has too much body now! We fixed the odor, but the texture is all wrong!"

Abigail sighed. "If it's not one thing, it's another."

"Maybe we should call the fire department," Todd said. "Just to be on the safe side."

"No need to bother them," replied Emma. "I just have to adjust the recipe a tad." She turned to her sister and smiled. "Back to work!"

Abigail nodded, then ushered us to the front hall. "Come again when you can stay for tea," she said as she opened the door.

I didn't need an invitation to leave. This house was not a safe place. Personally, I never wanted to set foot in there again.

"Those ladies scare me," I told Todd when we were out of earshot. I kept turning back, expecting a hand of smoke to chase us. But there were only the moon and the singing crickets.

"I don't think they like me," Todd said. It seemed to bother him.

I took a deep breath. "I think they're witches," I said quickly. I was sure that he was going to laugh at the idea.

But Todd just shrugged. "I don't know if I'd recognize a witch if I saw one. What *is* a witch anyway? At the very least, though, they must have a super-deluxe Mr. Wizard science kit hidden away. I've never seen smoke like that."

"What about the way they threw those eggs?" I asked.

I wanted to tell him about everything else—the bat, the voice, and the invitation to join the Witch Club of America. But I was just getting to know Todd. And he already thought I was strange. The last thing I needed was for him to think I was a *total* weirdo.

"The eggs have been puzzling me," he said, pushing his hair back. "I can't explain it. And I'm pretty good at scientific stuff. It's a mystery."

That's for sure, I thought. If he was looking for scientific explanations, he'd have to look real hard to explain the witches next door.

Later, alone in my room, I stared across at the Nightingales' house. Their windows were dark. But I half-expected some eerie glow to boil up from their basement.

Screech! It was their cockatoo, Harold. Good grief, but that bird was loud. And I was a whole house away!

"Cool it, Harold," I muttered to myself.

"Jenn-i-fer," Harold's voice called back, wavering in the air. *"Jenn-i-fer..."*

With a sigh, I jumped into bed, pulling the

covers to my nose. Harold's squawk wasn't as scary as the strange voice I'd been hearing. But believe me, it was no lullaby.

"You're next..." Harold screeched. "Next!"

I shivered.

"Dead..." he cackled. I gasped and buried my head under my pillow, but I couldn't block him out.

"Dead..."

6

Room of Doom

It was time for the room of doom.

My fingers gripped the cafeteria tray as I walked into the lunchroom. For me, this was the worst period at school. When you don't have any friends, there's nowhere to sit. And if you eat alone kids stare at you. It's enough to give you a stomachache.

"Hi," a voice said.

I turned and saw Kristy Geist smiling at me. She was sitting at a table with three other girls from our class.

"Hi," I muttered.

"Want to sit with us?" she asked.

For a second I thought she was kidding. Then she pulled out the empty seat beside her. The idea of sitting with some of the popular girls made me nervous, but I decided that it was now or never.

The girls were laughing about something Mr.

Suarez had done in English class. I smiled along with them as I ate my french fries. Maybe this popularity thing was easier than I'd thought.

"Hey, Jennifer!" Todd skidded over and straddled a chair down the table. "I've been thinking about that weird smoke, and I wanted to ask you something."

Not now! I glared at him.

"What are you talking about?" asked Kristy.

While I took a long sip of milk and stared down at my tray, Todd told the girls about the smoke that had swirled around the Nightingales's house last night. I braced myself for laughter. Instead, they were impressed.

"Cool!" Kristy said. "First the flying eggs, and now magic smoke. It must be fun living next door to the Nightingales," she said to me.

"Sure." I rolled my eyes. "You never know what they'll be cooking up next."

The girls laughed, and I felt a little better. Maybe there was hope for me here in Lake Trawley. Maybe Kristy would ask me to sit with them tomorrow, too.

Just then, a shadow crossed the table.

Chelsea's nose suddenly appeared in front of my face. "You're sssitting in my ssseat," she hissed through clenched teeth.

I shrugged. "Looked empty to me."

"Sit somewhere else, silly," Kristy told Chelsea. "Jen was just telling us about the Nightingales. They've got some new recipe that shoots off blue smoke."

"My mother says that they are certifiably insane." Chelsea tossed her lunch bag onto the table and gave me a nasty look. "And a health hazard. I hope you didn't touch them. You could catch something gross."

"Oh, Chelsea, give it a rest." Kristy rolled her eyes.

"As a matter of fact, I think Jennifer's looking a little green, isn't she?" Chelsea prodded.

The girls grew silent. Suddenly, I wanted to slide under the table and crawl away.

Kristy tried to defend me. "Leave her alone, Chelsea."

"Jen looks fine to me," Todd said.

"I don't know..." Chelsea made a big deal of staring at me. "Are those warts growing on your nose?"

Two of the girls snickered.

As usual, I couldn't think of anything to say. I took a bite of my burger. It tasted dry. I didn't want to eat another bite. But I couldn't get up and leave. That would be like surrendering.

"Did you hear what Bryan did in art class?" One of the girls launched into a story. But I tuned it all out and ate in glum silence.

Then something the Nightingales had said popped into my head. As I watched Chelsea slide a Twinkie into her mouth and lick her fingers, I realized that they were right. The thought was so funny I giggled out loud.

Chelsea frowned at me. "What's so funny?" she demanded.

"You know what?" I said. I couldn't believe the words came out of my mouth, but they did. "You *do* look like a snake!"

"What?" I stared in horror at my parents, certain I'd heard wrong.

"Violin lessons," my mother repeated with a big smile. "We've found the perfect teacher."

"I can't take any more lessons!"

Dad's brows pulled into a frown. We were in his den, where he'd been working over some briefs. "To make Junior Symphony you'll need to learn a second instrument—"

"I don't want to join Junior Symphony! Why can't I ever do what *I* want?"

They looked at me in shock, as if they couldn't believe what they were hearing.

"Jennifer..." Dad frowned. "Why didn't you say something before?"

"Really, Jennifer! We've already set up the

lessons," Mom said, sounding irritated. "Abigail is expecting you tomorrow afternoon."

Abigail! "You mean the witch next door?" I asked in horror.

Mom lowered her eyebrows. "That's a terrible thing to say."

"Abigail Nightingale used to be a fine violinist," Dad said. He smoothed back my hair, as if that would make everything all right. "I think you'll learn a lot from her."

I didn't want to learn how to play the violin. And I didn't want to go near the house next door ever again. How could I make my parents understand that I might not make it out alive?

"Can't you tell her that you changed your mind?" I asked. "I'm sure there's another violin teacher in town."

Mom shook her head. "Everything's set. And I don't want to hear another word about it."

I had no choice, as usual. So I marched away, pounded up the stairs, and slammed my bedroom door for good measure.

Harold screeched from next door. I opened the curtains and looked outside. It was dusk. Next door the windows glowed yellow, like cats' eyes.

At that moment I wished fervently that I *were* a witch. Then I'd take care of Chelsea...and zap my mother every time she tried to sign me up for another lesson...and make Megan move out to Oregon...In fact, I'd fix everything that was wrong in my life.

"Help...meeee..." Harold squawked.

"Oh, help yourself," I muttered, and slammed the window shut.

7

The Power

I was silent in the car on the way home from school the next day.

"Don't forget about your violin lesson at the Nightingales'," Mom said.

I didn't answer. And for once, my mother didn't press me. Maybe she felt bad. Or maybe she was dreaming up some other activity for me. Cooking lessons? Acrobatics? Who knew!

The last place I wanted to go was next door. But to tell the truth, after my run-in with Chelsea I was feeling gutsy. I had some questions for the witches. And this time I was going to get some answers.

If that didn't work, I was going to try to get a moment alone with Harold. Maybe I could get that grouchy cockatoo to talk to me.

Carrying my rented violin in its case, I headed next door.

"Over here, dear!" Emma waved at me from the side yard. I could barely make out the two silver heads and wrinkled faces amid the rosebushes.

"Emma's doing some pruning, since you and I won't have time," Abigail explained.

Emma held up a pair of sharp clippers and smiled. "I do love to chop, chop, chop!"

I stopped dead in my tracks. Was she talking about roses? Or something else?

With super speed, she started snipping. Withered blossoms fell around her like drops of blood. Then she sighed. "Ahh, but it is exhausting!"

"Ready for our lesson?" Abigail asked.

I shrugged.

"The violin is a beautiful instrument," Emma said. "I used to play it myself."

Abigail snorted. "You're tone deaf."

"But I did love to play," Emma added.

"Before we start the lesson, I have some questions," I said.

The sisters exchanged a smile.

"This is the moment we've been waiting for," Emma said proudly. "You want to know how to become a witch, don't you?"

"No," I said. "I want to know why you're picking on me. And why does that voice keep talking to me and making me do things? Am I possessed?"

"Oh, the Voice!" Emma said, as if it had a capital *V*. She touched one of her dimples. "I'd nearly forgotten."

"Possessed? Gracious, what a thought," said Abigail with a laugh.

"What has it been saying?" Emma asked.

"It calls my name. And it says 'We've come for you,'" I said. "And it sounds like a vicious little elf."

"Oh, my," said Abigail. "An elf? We're losing our touch, sister dear."

"Well," Emma pointed out, "we haven't used that trick for ages. I'm not surprised it's a bit rusty."

So the voice *was* their fault. I was beginning to get mad about this whole thing. It wasn't fair of them to use me for a little fun. "And how come *I* was chosen?" I snapped. "I mean, there are a lot of other girls around here who'd make better witches. Chelsea Stephens, for one."

Emma pressed a finger to her chin. "Oh, no, no, no. Chelsea would be a dreadful witch. She has a very small, mean heart. And no vision. Besides, she doesn't have the power."

"Well, neither do I!"

There was silence. The sisters looked at each

other, then turned their glowing blue eyes on me.

"No power?" Abigail asked. "Don't tell me you haven't felt it!"

Then it hit me. The power! I knew exactly what she meant.

There was the time when my fingers danced across the keyboard at the recital. And the time my legs rushed me up to the witches' front door to apologize. And yesterday, when that smoke was putting the squeeze on me, my arms had yanked it off like a champ.

"You mean—you mean that wasn't the Voice?" I quavered.

Abigail and Emma both gazed at me solemnly and shook their heads.

"What's happening to me?" I gasped.

"Not to worry, dear," said Emma gently.

"It's the power every witch possesses," Abigail explained. "A witch doesn't realize her power until she's about your age."

"And even then," added Emma, "she needs help to keep it under control. Witches' training. That's why we're here."

I shook my head. "But I don't want to be a witch."

"Jennifer," Abigail clucked, "there are some

things we cannot choose in life. You didn't choose your parents, did you?"

"Oh, I would have liked to have been born a princess." Emma sighed. "That would have been lovely, don't you think?"

Abigail gave her sister an exasperated look, then went on. "Like it or not, Jennifer, you're a special person with a passport to a special place. It's called the Shadow Zone. It's where magic comes from, and you're one of those people who can get there."

"Face it, Jennifer," Emma added. "You *are* a witch."

"Why did you come for me?" I asked. "Are you going to take me away from my parents?"

"Of course not." Abigail snorted. "It's time for us to train an apprentice, that's all."

"After three hundred years, a witch's power begins to fade," Emma explained.

Three hundred *years*? I gulped.

But Emma went on as if she had said nothing unusual.

"She needs to pass her skills on to an apprentice. Otherwise, the witch will fizzle into nothingness."

"And *I'm* the apprentice." I couldn't believe it. But after everything that had happened in the past few days, it made sense.

"Can I get a broomstick with a pearl handle?" I asked.

Abigail frowned. "Oh, now you're teasing us. Come inside and we'll prove our point."

"The proof is in the pudding!" Emma said as we crossed the yard.

I followed them into the living room. As we walked, I wondered what kind of proof they could show me. A diploma from witch school? A tall black hat?

Emma clapped her hands together. "I'll get the cup!" She disappeared into the kitchen and returned in the blink of an eye. She was holding a cup of the blue stuff I'd seen in the cauldron in the shed. Only this time it didn't smell or smoke. Yet.

"The cup," she said proudly.

"No thanks." I backed away.

"This isn't for you, Jennifer!" Emma giggled. "It's for Harold."

Slowly Emma lifted the cover of the bird's cage. The white cockatoo glared at her and snapped its beak.

"He's so cranky," Emma complained.

"Nasty," said Abigail. She held the cup up to the cage. "This is far too good for the likes of you, Harold."

I didn't say anything. After all, he was their pet. If they wanted to feed him this stuff, it was up to them.

Harold cocked his head and peered at the cup with one eye. Then he let out a screech.

"I knew he'd be difficult." Abigail snapped.

Emma nodded. "He's always been stubborn."

"Maybe he'd prefer water," I said.

"You try to feed him," Abigail urged me.

As much as I disliked the ill-tempered bird, I didn't want to poison him. "I don't think—"

"Go on!" Abigail urged. "I promise it won't hurt him. It's like a tonic."

"Please," Emma coaxed.

I looked from one sister to the other. As weird as they were, I didn't think they'd hurt Harold.

I took the cup from Emma. It was ice cold. Abigail lifted the latch, and Harold hopped awkwardly to the door. I nudged the cup under his beak.

He eyed me suspiciously. I half expected him to peck my fingers. Then, wonder of wonders, he dipped his beak into the drink.

Poof!

A gray cloud exploded in front of me, and I fell back. The cup clattered from my hand. I blinked rapidly, afraid of what I might see.

As the smoke cleared, a figure began to take shape. I gaped in surprise.

On the floor in front of me was a gangly, white-haired man with one foot caught in Harold's cage!

8

Frog Eyes and Newt Tails

I stumbled across the rose rug and fell into a big purple chair. My glasses slid down my nose, and I quickly pushed them back into place. I didn't want to miss a thing! The Nightingales' bird had turned into a man. A very *angry* man.

"Of all the tricks you've ever played on me, this takes the prize," he screeched. He yanked the birdcage off his foot and shook it. "I'm going to throw a spell on you that'll curl your toes!"

A spell! Was Harold a witch, too?

The sisters didn't seem alarmed.

"Oh, sit down, Harold. And stop that squawking." Abigail pointed to a chair.

"Such a cranky man," Emma said, sighing. She turned to Abigail. "We should have left him a cockatoo and donated him to the zoo!"

"A double spell!" Harold shouted, leaping to his feet. "No—a triple spell. That's what I'll throw on you."

"Pipe down," Abigail warned him. "After your life as a bird, I think you'll find that your powers have faded considerably."

Emma giggled. "Your squawk is worse than your bite!"

"A cockatoo!" Harold kicked the cage. "You have some nerve." He was just about to throw another tantrum when he noticed me.

"Jennifer," he whispered. His eyes narrowed to slits. Then he reached toward me.

"You leave her alone!" Abigail snapped.

Harold froze. But he continued to eye me as if I were his next meal.

"You're next," he told me, his fingers curling like claws.

"Get the rainbow dust!" Abigail told Emma, who floated off to the kitchen.

Harold's cold eyes flickered nervously as he slowly shrank away from me. "No tricks!" he shrieked.

"You're the one with tricks," Abigail said firmly. "I haven't forgotten what you did to Sarah."

"She looks like Sarah," Harold said, nodding at me.

Emma returned from the kitchen. "You're going to pay for what you did, you mean old bird."

What were they talking about? I wanted to ask, but I could see that Abigail was in no mood for questions. Harold had pushed her too far.

"We may be old," said Abigail, "but we still have a few spells up our sleeves."

Harold smoothed back his feathery white hair and scoffed. "I'd like to see you try one."

That did it.

Abigail narrowed her eyes and began to whisper, *"Frog eyes and newt tails, midnight shadows and dragon scales..."*

"Stop that!" Harold cried.

But Abigail's voice rose dramatically. *"A pinch of this, a taste of that, hairs from the ears of a big black cat!"* As she finished the verse, she shook her clenched fist in front of her. Then she opened her hand and blew on it, scattering rainbow-hued specks of dust.

The multicolored dust surrounded Harold. This time Harold froze for real, in mid-sneer.

"Well, that's that." Abigail wiped her hands.

I pushed my glasses into place and edged closer to him. "Is he still alive?"

"Of course, dear," Emma said. "The freeze will only last for a few hours."

"But by then, Harold will be on his way to a far-off place," Abigail said. "Let's see...I hear that Alaska is nice this time of year."

Emma nodded. "Oh, yes! They have long summer days when the sun never sets! Not a drop of darkness in twenty-four hours!"

Emma giggled. "Oh, Harold will like this vacation."

"How long was Harold a bird?" I asked.

"Oh, I don't know," Abigail said. "Two years, maybe. Or was it five?"

"You mean, you just zapped him and no one came looking for him?" I asked.

"Who would want to find Harold?" Emma answered. She had a point.

"Is he a witch, too?" I wanted to know.

Emma nodded. "A warlock. And not a very good one. Ever since he betrayed Sarah, no one would have anything to do with him. He was never invited to brew bashes, or cauldron cookouts, or even tea parties."

I was fascinated.

"But let's not let one bad warlock spoil our day," Abigail said. She was holding a violin case. "We need to get on with our lesson."

"Oh, right." Talk about a letdown!

It was hard to forget about spells and warlocks. And it would be even harder to ignore Harold, who stood stock-still in the corner. But I opened my violin case.

I expected Abigail to whip out a stack of sheet music and start the grandfather clock ticking like a metronome. But she took the violin and bow out of her violin case and put them on the marble table. Then she drifted over to the sofa and sat down.

"Join me over here, dear." She patted the spot next to her.

I took out my own violin and bow, and sat down beside her.

"Forgive me if I'm a little rusty," she said. "We'll start with something simple. Just relax and hold your instrument gently. See if you can follow along."

I waited for her to pick up the violin on the table. Instead, she pressed her hands to her forehead and closed her eyes. What was going on? Did she have a headache?

Then it started, sweet strains of music. But who was playing?

I turned and gasped. Abigail's violin was floating in mid-air! The bow glided over the strings, but no one was touching it. It was magic!

Emma sighed. "What a lovely song!"

Abigail opened one eye and peered at me. "Join in if you can."

My fingers gripped the neck of the violin. "But I don't even know how to hold it," I said.

"Do your best," said Abigail.

I tucked the bottom under my chin and stared over at the magic violin. Imitation was the key. First I copied its moves. Then the real magic happened.

My fingers came to life. They moved gently on the strings and stroked the bow with ease. I was playing along with the magic violin. And it wasn't hard. In fact, it felt pretty cool!

When the song ended, Emma applauded. "That was lovely!"

I couldn't help smiling. Maybe violin lessons weren't such a bad idea, after all.

That night, after I finished my homework, piano scales, and French exercises, I stretched out on my bed. The events of the afternoon played through my mind over and over. The Nightingales' words rang in my ears.

You are a witch.

The power...haven't you felt it!

Maybe it wouldn't be so awful to be a witch. I mean, if I could keep it quiet. The kids at school hadn't really warmed up to me yet. If anyone heard about this, I'd be the class clown for the rest of my life.

There was a strange noise outside my window. I scrambled off the bed and looked out, expecting to see colored smoke. Instead, I saw two silhouettes on the front porch next door. It was Emma and Abigail, and they were waving at something that hovered above them.

It looked like a man riding a pole. As the object rose in the air, I realized what—or rather, *who*—it was.

"Good-bye, Harold!" the sisters called.

The broomstick sailed high over the Nightingales' rooftop. It circled, then flew past my window with a *whoosh*.

I smiled, and wished him a good vacation in Alaska.

9

One-Way Broomstick

Math class was almost over, and everyone was getting restless.

Our teacher, Mrs. Turtle, was grading quizzes. Chelsea and Bryan were passing notes to each other. And I was chewing my pencil, figuring out a problem. As I wrote the answer, someone tapped me on the shoulder.

"Did you try out for the lip-synch contest?" It was Kristy, whispering across the aisle.

I shook my head. "Did you?"

She nodded. "I'm with a group of people. We've already started rehearsing."

"Good luck," I told her.

"You're going to need more than luck, Kristy," Chelsea added, butting in. "No one can win against me. My costume's almost done. It's so cool. With *green sequins*. I'm a sure winner."

I was surprised to hear Chelsea put down her

own best friend. But Kristy just let the whole thing drop.

After Chelsea turned away to write another note, Kristy asked me, "Want to eat lunch with us today?"

Weeks ago, it was all I'd wished for. But along with Kristy came Chelsea. It just wasn't worth the hassle.

"I—I can't," I stammered. "I have some homework to catch up on."

"Oh." Kristy's smile faded. Then she shrugged. "Maybe tomorrow."

"Maybe," I said.

"Maybe *not*," Chelsea broke in as the bell rang. "Nobody wants to sit next to a witch."

Why did she say things like that?

Right on cue, Bryan said, "What has blue hair, wears purple dresses, and flies at night?" He paused for dramatic effect, then belted out, "Grannies on a broomstick!"

Chelsea laughed while I picked up my knapsack and shoved past them. Good thing I'd made other plans.

I'd come up with a way to avoid the room of doom. Instead of following the pack to the lunchroom, I sneaked into the media center. I was safe there, at a table surrounded by walls of old books. No Chelsea. No problem finding a seat. And nobody stared at me because I was alone. In a library you're *supposed* to sit by yourself, nose in a book.

Of course, the plan had a few problems. For one, you're not supposed to eat in the library. And two, the food I'd stashed in my knapsack that morning wasn't too appetizing. Did you ever try to swallow a smashed slice of bread without milk? Not to mention the sticky raisins I had to pick off the bottom of the bag.

The lunch period was half over, and I was on my third book about Alaska. I was just popping a piece of crust into my mouth when someone came over.

Sure that Ms. Blundell had caught me, I shoved the bread into my mouth and looked up.

It was Todd.

"I've been looking all over for you!"

"Shh!" I glanced around nervously as he sat down at the table. "If you're not quiet, Ms. Blundell will give you a detention."

"She likes me." He shrugged, but dropped his voice to a whisper. "I saw the strangest thing last night. It shot right past my window."

"Really?"

"No propellers. No jet engine," he said, ticking off the science facts. "It was a flying broomstick! And someone was riding it."

I nodded.

"Can you believe it?"

I just kept nodding. "I saw it, too," I admitted.

"You did?" He was thrilled. "Then it *did* come from the witches' house!"

I stopped nodding. Todd was so excited about this whole witch thing. Why was it so easy for him to accept—and so hard for me?

That's when I decided to spill my guts. I told Todd everything. About the voice. About the bat. About Harold, the grouchy cockatoo who'd turned into a man. And most important, about the power I had.

Todd listened to every word. Then he had an idea. "I think we should go check out that cauldron in the shed."

"You do?" My voice squeaked in surprise. Did that mean he believed me?

"Definitely. A man turning into a bird...then back into a man again? It's amazing!" he said, a little too loud.

"Shh!" someone ordered.

Todd lowered his voice. "Think of the possibilities. Maybe the Nightingales don't even know the power of their potion. Do you realize what a chemical like that could do to our neighborhood? Or even to this country!"

I shrugged. "Even if we find the cauldron, what can *we* do about it?"

"We'd need to get a sample. Or at least a closer look..." The wheels of science were spinning in Todd's brain.

On the other hand, I was imagining the people of Lake Trawley turning into birds.

"So what do you say?" he asked.

"Guess we have to break into the shed and check out that cauldron," I agreed. "But don't blame me if the Nightingales turn us into parakeets!"

We waited until the sun had set, then met at the stone fence that backed up to the Nightingales' yard. I had to sneak past my parents, who thought I was doing homework. It made me feel guilty, but what I could tell them? That I was going out to spy?

A crescent moon hung just above the treetops. I could smell the roses, a scent so thick it reminded me of candy.

"I'll go first," Todd said.

"No," I insisted. "I know the way." I was a little scared. But I didn't want him to think I was a wimpy girl.

We cut through my backyard into the backyard next door. We crept past the kitchen door and around the corner. The shed was hidden in the shadows of the fir trees. Before I lost my nerve, I ran through the tall grass, toward trouble.

When we reached the door, I pushed up my glasses and studied the handle. The clasp was rusty, but it opened easily. "They don't even lock it."

"C'mon," Todd whispered. "Let's go inside."

I swallowed hard. The thought of the bubbling brew made my hands sweat. "Just keep away from the cauldron," I warned him. "Fall into that thing and you can kiss your life as a boy good-bye."

Todd nodded, and I pulled open the door. It creaked softly, eerily. My chest tightened. Slowly, we edged forward.

"Do you see it?" Todd whispered.

I shook my head. It was too dark. I blinked as my eyes adjusted.

The cauldron was gone! The musty shed looked tired and deserted. The only things inside were an old clothes wringer, a butter churn, and some cracked picture frames.

"What happened to the cauldron?" I said, scratching my head.

Todd peered over my shoulder. "Looks like it's time for a garage sale."

"They must have moved it," I said. "The Nightingales *know* things—it's like ESP or something. They probably sensed that we were coming. So they took the cauldron into the house. That's got to be it."

Todd shrugged. "I guess we'll have to check the house."

"Didn't you hear what I just said?" I whispered. "They have strange powers. We can't snoop around their house. It's dangerous."

As we left the shed, I could tell Todd was disappointed. I felt the same way. I knew Todd believed my stories about the witches. But it wouldn't have hurt to have some proof—like a bubbling cauldron.

I had just closed the shed door when Todd grabbed my arm and pointed at the back of their house. "A light just flickered in the back. Let's take a look."

We crept back behind the house. The light was coming from the kitchen. Through the window I could see Emma and Abigail at the stove. Emma held an oil lamp in each hand. The window sill was too high to see what was going on. And the closer we got, the less we could see.

Abigail was talking, but we couldn't hear the words. Creeping closer, I strained to catch the conversation. No such luck.

"We need something to climb on," I whispered.

Todd hauled an old wooden crate over to the house. He put it under the window, and I climbed up. Now I could see and hear what was going on.

"Good riddance," Abigail was saying. "He'll have a long vacation up north. *After* he recovers from his one-way broomstick ride."

They were talking about Harold!

"Such a grouchy man, and a foul bird to boot," Emma clucked.

I motioned for Todd to climb up beside me. He had to hear this.

Todd stepped up next to me. Together, we leaned to one side of the window frame, trying to hear without being seen.

"One question remains, sister dear," said Abigail.

"Oh, dear." Emma sighed. "What *shall* we do with Jennifer?"

Just then the box tipped. With a cry, I grabbed for the sill, holding tight till I was steady.

Todd's arms flailed behind me as he teetered forward, then fell back. His motion set me off-balance a second time.

"Whoa—whoa!" I cried, falling to the ground.

"Who's there?" Emma threw open the window.

Abigail snorted. "Is it a burglar?"

They both leaned out the window, peering into the darkness.

We might have gotten away with it if Todd hadn't chosen that moment to sneeze. But he did, and the witches looked down.

I wished I could blend into the grass.

"Oh, my," Emma clucked. "What have we here?"

Feeling like a traitor, I sneaked a look up at them.

"Spies," Abigail said, rubbing her hands together. "Emma, what shall we do with them?"

"I'm afraid we have no choice," Emma said. "We must have them for dessert."

10

Hocus Pocus

Fear shadowed Todd's face. "What do you mean...*have* us for dessert?"

I was wondering the same thing. I mean, we weren't *that* sweet, were we?

"Dessert tonight is crumpets and tea," Emma replied.

"You'll catch your death of cold in the wet grass," Abigail said, frowning down at us. "Come along inside where it's warmer." Without waiting for an answer, she shut the window.

Todd and I looked at each other. I could tell he was dying of curiosity.

"Oh, all right," I said. "But don't eat anything!"

Todd brushed the grass off his pants and grinned. We walked to the kitchen door and Abigail opened it for us.

"Thanks," I said politely. "But Todd's not hungry—and neither am I. We both just ate."

"Jennifer," said Abigail, "I'm disappointed in you. You still don't understand. Rule number one for witches is that you must trust your own kind."

I nudged Todd and gave him a look that said, *Get a load of this.*

Todd was fascinated. "Jennifer's a witch?"

"An apprentice," Abigail corrected.

"A student of witchcraft," Emma added.

Todd covered his mouth to hide a grin. I didn't think it was so funny.

"You mean, she's in training?" Todd asked.

"Exactly," said Abigail. "Now just make yourselves comfortable while we brew the tea."

I sat down beside Todd and stared at the cups and saucers. There was no way I was going to eat anything. And I wasn't going to let Todd eat anything, either.

"So, what do witches do?" Todd asked curiously.

"We help keep order," Abigail told him. "When things get out of balance, we fix them."

"We're cosmic police!" Emma giggled.

"Why did you pick Jennifer?" he asked. "Because she lives next door?"

"Oh, goodness, no!" Abigail laughed. "We moved next to Jennifer on purpose."

"We've been looking for you," Emma twittered, smiling at me. "Your great-great-great-great-grandmother was a dear friend of ours!"

"I think you're missing a 'great,'" Abigail corrected her.

My head reeled. "You mean, one of my ancestors was a—a—"

"Witch!" they both cried in delight.

"Cool!" Todd said.

I was doomed.

Dazed, I watched as Emma placed the plate of crumpets on the table and poured a thin caramel syrup over the top. The sweet smell made my mouth water. When Abigail set the teapot beside it, I caught a whiff of cinnamon and spice.

No treat ever looked so good.

Don't eat anything! I mouthed the words to Todd. He eyed the plate of crumpets and sighed.

Emma and Abigail didn't appear to notice. They served four plates and four cups. I tell you, it was all I could do not to reach for that stuff, too. But then I remembered what had happened to Harold.

Holding tightly onto Todd's arm, just in case he should try for a crumpet, I said, "I've never heard of anyone in my family being a witch."

Abigail pursed her lips. "It's not something people advertise. Look what happened to Sarah."

"Sarah?" I asked.

"Your distant grandmother," Emma explained patiently.

"What happened to her?"

"Oh, my!" Emma's hand fluttered to her throat. "She doesn't know."

"Of course not," Abigail snapped. "It was a long time ago."

"How long have you been witches?" Todd asked.

"Three hundred years. Or is it four now?" Emma asked her sister.

They conferred. "Around three hundred and seventy" was Abigail's final answer. "Give or take a few years."

"We're trying to retire," Emma confided. "Our powers began to fade in the last century. That's why we need you, Jennifer."

"You seem pretty powerful to me." I remembered the way Abigail had put Harold into that trance.

Suddenly, Todd shook my arm off. In a flash he stabbed a crumpet with his fork and shoved the whole thing into his mouth.

I leaped from my chair in a panic. I had to save him. I couldn't let him turn into a bird!

"Something wrong, dear?" Emma asked.

"Wait! Don't—" I grabbed Todd as he happily chewed the crumpet. "Don't swallow!" I snatched his plate away and stared at him, waiting for something awful to happen.

"I bat chew maggot!" Todd said over a mouthful.

"What?" He wasn't making sense. I bit my lips, waiting for him to sprout feathers.

Todd swallowed, then repeated, "I had to have it. I wanted to see what it would be like to change into a bird."

"A bird?" Abigail said icily.

"Isn't Todd going to turn into a cockatoo—like Harold?" I turned to Emma.

Emma straightened in her chair. "Goodness, Mr. Calavicci wouldn't be a cockatoo. And certainly not from crumpets. You're thinking of a transformation, dear. For that, we'd need our special brew, which we don't serve up every day."

"Special brew?" I asked. Now we were getting somewhere. "Was that what I saw boiling in the shed? The blue stuff I fed Harold?"

"Not *that* brew." Emma giggled.

"Here's a quick lesson, Jennifer," Abigail said. "Blue mixtures end spells. Rainbow mixtures begin them. Our favorite spell is mixed into our true self drink mix. We call it True Brew—"

"With ten percent real fruit juice," Emma added. "We were just about to make some more."

"But we had to move it from the shed," said Abigail. "We weren't sure if we could trust Mr. Calavicci. And we knew you two would pay us a visit."

"But now we've seen he's pure of heart." Emma smiled at Todd.

"How did you move the cauldron?" I asked. "It had to be heavy."

"Minor levitation. A simple trick," Abigail answered. "Silly hocus-pocus."

"Why did you ask me to move those boxes in the basement?" I asked. "You could have done the job yourselves."

"Oh, we were just testing your courage."

"The same with the smoke," Emma said. "We had to know if you were worthy."

They made it sound so *normal!* I couldn't believe we were talking about whether or not I would be a good witch!

Todd lifted his teacup and stared at the brown liquid inside. "Is there True Brew in this?"

"Oh, no, no, no," Emma said. "You'd be able to see the color. Or rather, the many colors."

"And of course, we only use True Brew on

people who need it," Abigail explained.

"Like Harold?" I asked.

"Oh, Harold!" Emma made a tsk-tsk sound. "He was always cranky. And being a bird did not improve his mood."

"Does True Brew turn people into animals?" Todd asked.

"Into their true self," Abigail corrected. "Whatever that may be."

Emma clapped a hand to her mouth. "Abigail, do you remember that wicked little boy who watched too much television? *Poof!* He turned right into a couch potato!"

The sisters collapsed into laughter. Suddenly I remembered what had happened that day when everything seemed fuzzy, and I felt so tiny. "So you really did turn me into a mouse," I said. "With those drops of True Brew!"

"Oh, *we* didn't choose the mouse part." Abigail shook her head. "You were feeling small and weak. The brew just revealed your true self at that moment—a mouse."

"You mean, True Brew doesn't always turn you into the same thing?" I asked.

"You don't feel like a mouse anymore, do you?" Abigail prodded.

I blinked. She was right. I felt stronger. More in control. And more my true self.

"Didn't you stand up to your parents about the violin lessons?" Abigail reminded me.

"But it didn't do any good."

"Oh, you'd be surprised," Emma said, winking over the rim of her teacup.

"And you showed a smidgen of nerve with Chelsea," Abigail said.

"Just a little," I said, remembering that day at the lunch table. But since then, I'd been trying to avoid her. There was still a bit of mouse left in me.

I looked from one sister to the other. It was hard to imagine them hanging out with one of my long-dead relatives. "I can't believe my distant grandmother was a witch."

"It's true," Abigail said, a sad expression softening the wrinkles of her face. "If only we could have done something."

"Too bad Harold snitched on her," Emma added.

"What did he do?" Todd asked.

The sisters exchanged a look, then started clearing away the tea things.

"Some things are better left unsaid." Abigail took the teapot over to the counter, then touched my shoulder. "The most important thing is that we begin your training."

"It's our top priority," Emma said. "If we don't take on an apprentice soon, we'll be finished." She snapped her fingers. "Fizzled!"

"I'm just not ready," I said. "It's all so weird."

Abigail nodded. "Think hard. But don't delay. Our time is running out..."

11

Into the Fire

When I got home the house was quiet. Mom was reading in her room. Dad was in the den. They hadn't even realized I was gone.

I had homework to do. But something the witches had said really bugged me. "Dad..." I pushed open the den door.

My father looked up when I came in. "Hey, Jen. Something on your mind?"

"Sort of. I've got some questions. I was hoping you could help me."

"Fire away."

I perched on the edge of a chair and chewed at my lower lip. "Was there ever a witch in our family?"

Dad peered at me. I think he was wondering where I'd gotten this information. But instead of acting as if I were crazy, he said, "So, you heard about that, did you?"

My mouth dropped open. "It's true?"

"Ever heard of the Salem Witch Trials? They took place back in 1692, three hundred years ago. A few women were burned at the stake because people thought they were witches. One of your mother's great-great-grandmothers was among them."

"Burned at the stake..." My mouth was dry. "Do you know her name?"

"Sarah something-or-other. Why?"

Sarah! The Nightingales had been right!

"Jennifer!" Dad was alarmed. "You're white as a ghost!"

I shook my head. "It's okay. I gotta go practice piano, or French, or something." My mind raced as I stumbled out of the den. It was true! Every word!

So I wasn't the first one in this family to have *powers.* I thought of Sarah, and I shuddered. She'd been killed because she was a witch. I knew that people didn't burn witches at the stake anymore, but even so I would have to be careful. Very careful.

"Jennifer?" My mother stopped me in the hallway.

"Don't worry. I'll practice piano tonight," I mumbled.

"And the violin," she reminded me. "Junior Symphony tryouts are this week."

"Right," I muttered. Since I'd started the lessons with Abigail, I'd actually enjoyed the violin. But auditions were the last thing on my mind right now.

I was a witch! It was in my blood. And there was nothing I could do about it.

The next day at school, I decided to jump from the frying pan into the fire. I wasn't going to hide out in the library at lunchtime anymore. Jennifer the mouse was coming out of her hole in the wall. From now on, I was going to be Jennifer the girl.

I walked straight into the lunchroom and got on line. After days of crumbled bread and bruised bananas, tuna surprise never looked so good!

"Sit here!" Kristy called out, waving to me.

My tray landed on the table beside her, and I dug into the food. The other girls—Maria and Stephanie—were joking about a cute boy they'd seen at Here's the Beef. I laughed along. It was sort of fun.

But I knew it wouldn't last.

Chelsea slithered up to the table and took the chair beside mine. She eyeballed my books and violin case, and I could feel what was coming. Time to pick on the Junior Symphony dweeb.

"Taking violin lessons?" she asked. "Or is that a case for your broomstick?"

"Get with the program," I told her. "We witches fly on 747s."

That shut her up, at least for a minute. There was no winning against a girl like Chelsea. But I had to give it my best shot.

We all stood around the cauldron in the shed—Emma, Abigail, Todd, and I. The multicolored liquid was simmering, but the witches had asked Todd and me to stir it.

"It seems to be sticking a tad on the bottom," Emma said.

Standing clear of the overflowing bubbles, Todd pushed the giant wooden spoon. "If Jennifer becomes an apprentice, will she learn how to make this magic potion?"

"True Brew," Abigail corrected him. "And yes, it's something every witch should know."

"It's just one tool of witchcraft," Emma explained. "There are so many tricks. I love them all!"

"It scares me," I admitted. "I mean, what if I gave it to the wrong person?"

"Pish-posh!" Abigail waved off the question. "Jennifer, sometimes you worry too much."

"But being a witch can be dangerous," I said.

"My dad told me about my distant grandmother, Sarah. You didn't tell me she was burned for being a witch."

Todd looked up from the brew. "Is that true?"

Abigail and Emma exchanged a look.

"It was all Harold's fault," Emma said.

Abigail nodded. "Sarah was put on trial because Harold told everyone she was a witch."

"But Harold's a warlock," I pointed out. "He could have been burned, too."

"True," said Emma. "But his witchcraft is weak. The man never had formal training. And he's always resented us because our powers are stronger. That's why he betrayed Sarah."

"What a creep," Todd said.

"Good thing he's tucked away in Alaska," I said. He'd said that I looked like Sarah. I shivered.

"The Great White North." Abigail sighed. "Perhaps Harold will learn a thing or two."

"Let's hope so," Emma agreed. Then she pulled out a little gold watch on a chain and peered at it. "Anyone for tea?"

"As long as it's tea, and not True Brew," Todd said as he pulled the giant spoon out of the cauldron.

"I could use a strong cup," Abigail said.

"That sounds lovely," Emma agreed. "Let's go

back to the house and have it there."

While the witches made tea, I practiced the violin. Junior Symphony tryouts were tomorrow, and I was a little nervous about it.

Todd watched in amazement. I guess he'd learned to play trombone the hard way.

"The kettle's on," Emma sang.

"Along with crumpets for four!" Abigail added. "Now! Back to that violin lesson."

For once, I didn't mind playing with an audience. Everyone watched as my fingers danced over the strings in tandem with the magic violin.

When we finished the piece, everyone clapped. The magic violin tipped in the air, taking a bow.

"That's the coolest," Todd said. "Can you teach me the trombone that way?"

Abigail frowned. "Sorry, young man. I've just never been a fan of the brass section. If you—"

She was interrupted by the sound of Mom's voice calling. "Jennifer..."

Emma hurried to the door to let my mother in. "Have you come for tea?" she asked brightly.

"Well, no..." Mom turned to me. "It's time for Jennifer's French lesson."

Mom beamed when Todd said hello. All she saw was the star of Junior Symphony. What would she think if she knew that Todd and I talked about witches and brew instead of notes and measures?

"I forgot all about French," I said. "Can we postpone it?" I cast a hopeful glance at my mother, who shook her head.

"When would we squeeze it in?" Mom pointed out. "You're booked solid, young lady. And you have symphony tryouts tomorrow."

"Come on into the kitchen," Abigail invited Mom. "We've just set the table."

"I'd love to..." Mom smiled. "But we can't keep Mrs. Devereaux waiting."

"Nonsense," Abigail said. "Now, Elaine, how do you like your tea?"

"With milk," said Mom, "but I don't want to trouble you."

"No trouble at all!" Emma glided off.

As we filed into the kitchen, I sensed that more was brewing than just tea. Clearly, the Nightingales had something up their lavender sleeves.

Mom checked her watch. "We can't stay long," she murmured, dropping into a chair. "How are the violin lessons going?"

"The violin can be a lovely instrument," Abigail said, "in the right hands."

That made me think of the magic violin. I

covered my mouth to hide a giggle, and Todd cracked a smile.

"But how many lessons can one girl squeeze in?" Emma asked.

"Piano, violin, tennis, and French..." Mom patted my shoulder. "Our Jen's getting to be quite accomplished."

"Tea's ready." Abigail's blue eyes flashed behind her glasses. "Can you spare the time?"

"Just for one cup," Mom said.

"But Mom—" I wanted to get her out of there before Emma and Abigail decided to "fix" Mom's busy life.

"Jennifer..." The stress was clear in Mom's voice. "Where are your manners?"

Maybe I was overreacting. I tried to sit politely at the table. Just a few days ago, it had been easy for me to keep quiet as a mouse.

Emma and Abigail served up their crumpets and tea. I folded my hands and smiled as Mom and Emma laughed over a joke.

Then my eyes fixed on the multicolored syrup that streamed out of the teapot spout. Tiny bubbles rose from the cups.

That was no tea!

"Don't!" I screamed as Mom lifted a cup to her lips and took a gulp of True Brew!

12

You Are What You Eat

"Stop!" I shouted. "Please stop!"

Mom froze. Her cheeks were puffed out from holding the liquid in her mouth.

Then she swallowed.

Poof!

"No!" I cried, shielding my eyes from the smoke. The air was still thick with mist when I felt a nudge on my arm. I looked down and saw that it was a ram, prodding me.

"Mom?" I touched the top of the animal's head, but it just bleated and nudged me again. "Aw, Mom..." My eyes filled with tears.

Todd was stunned. "You gave True Brew to Jennifer's mom?"

"And now she's a ram," I said, choking on the words. I turned on Emma and Abigail. *"How could you?"*

At first the sisters seemed surprised. They didn't understand why I was upset.

Then Emma's pale face softened. "People are what they are, dear," she said. "And she's not just a ram, she's a *battering* ram."

"How appropriate," Abigail observed. "True Brew always gets it right, although this particular transformation is a play on words. Just look at how she keeps prodding you."

Emma clucked in agreement. "She doesn't know when to stop."

"Don't say that," I cried.

"But it's the truth, dear," Abigail said firmly. "And it was true when she was a person."

That truth was now butting me in the arm. In a minute, the ram would push me out of my chair. There was no ignoring my mother, as usual.

"Would you cut it out?" I said to the the ram. I tried to push its head back, but it just started nudging my hand, as if it were all a game.

"You never give up, do you?" I said. I looked into the ram's eyes and saw my mom blink back at me.

"That was a rotten trick," Todd told the sisters.

I turned to the Nightingales, who were quietly sipping their tea. "You've got to turn her back into a person. Please," I pleaded.

Abigail frowned. "Do you think she's learned

from this brief glimpse of her true self?"

The ram bleated and pressed against my leg. The poor thing just couldn't hold still. "I don't know," I admitted. "But I can't let my mom stay this way."

"It would be a pity to cut the lesson short," Abigail said.

"But time is relative in these things," Emma added. "After all, Harold was a cockatoo for years, and he *never* learned from his true self."

"True." Abigail sighed, then nodded at me. "Do as you wish."

"We'll hope for the best," Emma said. Out of thin air she produced a baby bottle filled with what looked like blue milk

"Come on, Mom!" I said as I pushed the bottle toward her. "Don't be so hard-headed."

Poof!

My mother sat in the chair beside me, acting as if nothing at all had happened. "What's in this?" she asked with a dizzy smile, examining the cup of tea.

"Mom?" I had never been so relieved to see her.

"Do you like our blend?" Abigail asked.

"The flavor is familiar," Mom went on. "Like mint and...berries."

"Ten percent real fruit juice," Emma said,

with her hands sweetly folded.

Just then Mom snapped back into her busy mode. She checked her watch. "Look at the time." She jumped up so fast, she nearly spilled her tea. "We'd better go."

"I'll meet you outside," I told her. "I just have to get my violin."

"Make it quick," Mom said. She grabbed her purse and went out the front door with a hurried "good-bye."

I spun around and faced the Nightingales. "I can't believe you would do that to my mother."

"But, dear, she batters you like a ram," Emma said softly. "We were just trying to help."

"I'll fix my own problems." Tears rolled under my glasses as I stormed into the living room and packed up my violin.

Todd and the Nightingales followed, keeping a safe distance behind me. The witches didn't need to read my mind to know that I was steaming mad.

"You'd better find another apprentice," I said, grabbing my violin case. "Because I can't do that to people. I'll never be a witch. Never!"

No one said a word as I marched out, letting the door slam shut behind me.

13

Misery

I was miserable.

That night I tossed in bed, trying to chase the witches out of my mind. But it was useless.

On the one hand, I was disappointed. The fact that I was a witch had been growing on me. I was fascinated by the power, that weird force that sprang to life at the oddest times. And I actually *liked* the witches next door.

On the other hand, I didn't know if I was cut out to be a witch. Power is a scary thing. That reality hit me hard when I saw what True Brew did to my mom.

I wanted spells that rhymed, fairy dust, and floating teapots, not more problems. I had enough of those!

Of course, I overslept the next morning. I barely had time to shovel down my cornflakes and brush my teeth. When I started out the door without my violin, my mother got upset.

"What's wrong with you?" she said, handing me the case. "Junior Symphony tryouts are this afternoon, and you're walking around in a daze."

If only she knew.

The final bell was ringing as I ran up the school steps. It was going to be a rotten day.

At lunchtime I braved the cafeteria. Todd was already sitting with Chelsea, Kristy, and their friends. I dropped my books and violin case onto the table. "Will you watch this stuff while I stand in line?"

"No problem," Todd said. I could feel his eyes on me as I walked away. We hadn't talked since I'd stormed out of the Nightingales' house. I wondered what he thought of me as now. A coward? A quitter? Or just a party pooper?

By the time I got back to the table, Chelsea had scarfed down her sandwich. "No time for witchy fun," she said, rolling her lunch bag into a ball. "Gotta run!"

Too cute for words. I watched her carefully as she sprang out of her seat and joined Bryan at another table.

"Sit down," Kristy tugged on my sleeve. "I've been waiting for you. There's something I wanted to ask you and Todd."

Please don't ask about the witches, I thought.

"Shoot," said Todd.

"Tomorrow's the lip-synch contest," Kristy said. "We're doing 'Surfin' U.S.A.'"

Todd nodded. "Good choice."

I felt a twinge of remorse that I hadn't had the nerve to audition for the biggest event in middle school. Oh, well. There was always next year. "Good luck," I told Kristy.

"The thing is, two kids in our group are out with the flu." She looked from Todd to me, then went on. "Would you, um, could you guys take their places?"

I was speechless. Kristy had asked *me* to be in her group!

"I'll do it if Jen does it," Todd said, looking at me.

"Well, sure," I said. "Sounds like fun. What do we have to do?"

"Great!" Kristy's face lit with a smile. "We're all meeting backstage..." She gave us the details. I was surprised to hear that Chelsea was *not* included and said so.

"Oh, she's doing a solo act," Kristy said. I glanced across the room. Chelsea and Bryan were fighting over a portable computer game.

"We're competing *against* Chelsea?" I asked.

"I know. Scary, huh?" Kristy rolled her eyes, and we all laughed.

After the girls went off to their lockers, Todd

and I stayed at the table to talk.

"Abigail and Emma were pretty upset yesterday," he told me. "They said you missed the point of True Brew."

I felt like a star pupil who'd failed a lesson. "I understand it. But they shouldn't have turned my mom into a ram. I can stand up to my mother on my own. I don't need magic."

Silence. I waited for Todd to say, *Then deal with her, already!* But he just nodded.

"I know the True Brew upset you," he said. "But still, I'd like to try a shot of that stuff on my mom. Maybe she'd stop nagging me to clean my room."

"I don't think that's what True Brew is intended for," I said sternly.

Todd groaned. "You sound just like Emma and Abigail."

"Shh..." The last·thing I needed was for someone to hear us talking about witches.

"Sorry. Anyway, you've changed, Jen. Witch or not, you're coming out of your shell."

"Yeah, well, I'm doing my best," I said with a shrug. But I knew he was right. Even Chelsea didn't scare me anymore as she slithered past with a sly look on her face. She actually smiled at me as she left the lunch room.

What was she up to?

"We'd better get going," Todd said, pushing his chair back.

I stood up and gathered my books. As I glanced down at the table, I realized something was missing.

It wasn't on any of the chairs. It wasn't on the floor. It wasn't anywhere.

"What's wrong?" Todd asked.

"My violin...it's gone!"

14

Vanished!

"I can't believe it," Todd said, peering under the table. "It was here with your books when you got on line. I saw it, right here."

"My mother's going to kill me," I said. "Junior Symphony tryouts are today, after school. Mr. Chong will be really impressed when I show up with no violin!"

"It's got to be around here," Todd said. "Violins just don't get up and walk away—"

"Unless they're magic," I said.

He stared at me. "You don't think that—"

I shook my head. "No. My violin was just a rental. Looks to me like somebody swiped it when I wasn't looking."

We did one more sweep of the area, but there was no sign of my violin. There was something fishy, though. I remembered the way Chelsea had acted as she left the cafeteria. I sensed that she had something to do with this, but without proof I couldn't accuse her.

"What are you going to do?" Todd asked me.

"I'm not sure." My parents had their hearts set on me making it into the symphony. And to be honest, I wanted to get in, too. Not **just to** make Mom and Dad happy, but because I really did like playing violin.

"Maybe it'll turn up before the end of the day," Todd suggested.

"Maybe. I'll check the Lost and Found after school."

The rest of the afternoon dragged like ketchup that won't come out of the bottle. When I checked the office after school, the secretary told me what I already knew. No violins had been turned in.

Unless I could produce a violin out of thin air, I was in big trouble. Not only because of Junior Symphony tryouts, but also because a violin could be very expensive to replace.

The shrill noise of tuning instruments filled the air as I plodded down the hall. The moment of truth. I would have to come clean with Mr. Chong, the music teacher. Later, much later, I'd deal with my parents.

Kids and instruments and open cases filled the cavernous pit in the music room. I tiptoed through the mess toward Mr. Chong

It would have been easy to turn around, run home, and just tell my mother that I didn't make the cuts. But I wanted this for me. I had to give it my best shot, even if it did require some courage.

Mr. Chong tapped his baton against one hand as I explained the whole story. "You should be more careful," he said. "A musician always takes care of her instrument."

"I know, sir. Is there any way I can still try out?" My voice sounded thin, but at least I got the words out. "How about tomorrow?"

"That's impossible," he said. "We're making up the final list today."

My heart was in my throat. I was going to blow it. "What if I borrowed someone else's violin?"

He shrugged. "If you can work it out, we'll let you keep your audition time."

"Thanks," I said. I desperately searched the faces around me. Two boys in the violin section were tuning up. I walked over and started talking to them. But when they heard what I wanted, they shied away.

"This is my father's violin," one kid said. "He made me promise not to let anyone touch it."

The other kid agreed. "You might knock it out of tune."

I went down the row to a girl with braces and straight blond hair. She smiled when I told her my name.

"My name's Susan," she said. "And you don't have to explain. I heard you talking to Mr. Chong. Someone swiped your violin, right?" When I nodded, she frowned. "That's awful. But I'll lend you mine."

Bingo!

As I sat at the dinner table with my parents that night, the tension was so thick you could cut it with a knife.

My audition had gone okay, thanks to the violin that Susan had lent me. But I still didn't make it into Junior Symphony.

"I'm just so disappointed," Mom said. "Symphony would have been so good for you."

"Mom—" I put down my fork. "I wanted it, too. But sometimes things just don't work out." I hadn't even told them about the missing violin. That news could wait another day.

"There's always next year," I went on. "Mr. Chong says I need more experience. But the point is, you have to back off. Let *me* decide what I want to do with my time."

"She's right, Elaine," Dad said quietly. "I think that Jennifer's old enough now to make some of her own decisions."

Mom squeezed the fringe on her placemat. "I don't mean to push so hard," she admitted. Her brown eyes were wide as she peered at me. "It's just that, when I was your age, my parents couldn't afford lessons. I wanted you to have the chance to do all the things I never had a shot at."

I frowned. "That's nice, but—"

"I think we've given Jennifer a good start," Dad said. "And now it's time to let her grow up a little."

Mom sighed. "Okay. I guess you're right." She turned to me. "Does this mean you're dropping violin?"

"No. But I've had it with French lessons."

"Fine," said Mom. "I'll call Mrs. Devereaux in the morning."

"And there's one more thing." I wanted to break the other news gently. "There's this lip-synch contest at school tomorrow, and I, well, I'm going to be in it."

My parents exchanged a look. I gritted my teeth, waiting for their disapproval.

Instead, Mom smiled. "Good for you, Jen," she said. "What song are you doing?"

"'Surfin' U.S.A.,'" I said tentatively.

"No kidding?" Dad beamed. "Your mom and I used to dance to that song all that time."

"'Tell the teacher we're surfin'...'" Mom sang in a silly voice that made us all laugh.

"So I'm not one of the Beach Boys," Mom said. Then she asked me what time the competition began. When I filled my parents in on the details, they decided to change their schedules around so they could come watch.

Go figure, I thought as I finished off my peas and carrots. My parents weren't as stubborn as I'd thought. I just needed to hold my ground when they pushed me too hard.

Friday dawned bright and blue. I dressed in jeans and a T–shirt, then pulled on a loose blue V-necked sweater. Tucked inside my knapsack were a pair of flowered shorts and bright yellow sandals. I was going to lip-synch my way to the top of the charts and dress the part, too.

I was on my way to the bus stop when I heard a frail voice call out. "Jennifer..."

The Nightingales stood in their rose garden, waving in unison. Their big straw sun hats bobbed in the breeze. I stared down at the weeds as I plodded through their yard.

We hadn't talked since the day I'd stormed out of their house. Looking back, I realized that I'd been kind of a jerk. Turning into a ram hadn't hurt Mom at all. But it had taught me that

I couldn't let her push me into things all the time.

"Hi," I said. "Sorry about the other day."

"And we're sorry about your audition," Emma said. "Better luck next year, dear."

"Did Mom tell you?" I asked.

"Oh, no," Abigail said, clipping a dead rose. "You'd be surprised at what we can tune in on our TV sets."

Emma beamed. "Much more interesting than soap operas, dear. I got so mad when that Chelsea Stephens swiped your violin."

"She did?" I blinked. "You *saw* that?"

Abigail nodded. "Pushed it under the lunch table and passed it off to Bryan, that loud boy. He took it into the school kitchen and stuffed it into the pantry. You'll find it there, next to the canned tomatoes."

"I thought it was Chelsea," I said. "But I didn't realize she had an accomplice."

"Case closed," Emma said smugly.

"Thanks for the tip," I said. "I've got to deal with Chelsea, once and for all." As I spoke, I noticed something flickering on the Nightingales' lavender skirts. I adjusted my glasses for a better look. But as my eyes focused, I didn't believe what I was seeing.

The sisters were becoming transparent, like a

tinted sheet of sandwich wrap. I could see roses bobbing behind them!

"Something wrong, dear?" Emma asked.

"You seem to be...fading," I said.

Abigail looked down and gasped. "We're losing power!"

"It's the fizzle!" Emma cried. "We're fizzling fast!"

15

Fizzling Fast!

Alarmed, Abigail dropped her pruning shears.

Emma brushed her skirt, as if a few good swipes could fix the problem. "Oh, dear! Abigail, what can we do?"

"There's nothing to be done," Abigail replied. "We failed to pass on our powers. Now it's too late."

"This is my fault!" I cried. "If I'd agreed to be your apprentice, you wouldn't be fizzling. But I—I just don't know what to do!"

"Emma," Abigail gasped, "we may be able to stall the fizzle. Close your eyes and focus."

"Oh, dear!" Emma cried. "There's barely any of me left to concentrate."

"Think of solid things," Abigail said weakly. *"Pillars of salt and mountains high..."* But before she could finish, her voice wavered.

Suddenly, my lips felt rubbery. The power! It was back. I finished the spell as Abigail's voice faded. *"Granite rocks and fat mud pies, a lump of coal, a slab of stone, iron weights, and dinosaur bones!"*

I snapped my fingers, and a puff of blue dust shimmered through the air. When the air cleared, Emma and Abigail were standing before me, solid as ever.

"Oh, what a relief!" Abigail sighed.

"Good job, Jennifer!" Emma said.

I shrugged. "You had me scared there. Do you feel okay?"

The witches nodded.

"But it's just a temporary spell," Abigail explained. "You can't defy the law of witches. We must find an apprentice soon."

Emma nodded sadly. "We've been avoiding the search, hoping you'd change your mind."

"I wish I could," I said. "But it still scares me. How do you know whether or not something is the right thing to do?"

"Trust your heart."

It was that voice again.

"Very funny," I told the witches.

They blinked, confused. "Did we miss something?" Abigail asked.

I wasn't about to let them start the voice thing again, but before I could object, Emma changed the subject. "We have a little gift just for you, dear," she said brightly.

"A token of good luck," Abigail explained. "We're tickled pink about your contest."

"The lip-synch?" How did they know? They must have seen previews on their magic television.

"Here you go!" Emma held up a plastic pouch of colored crystals. They sparkled as she placed the bag in the palm of my hand.

"True Brew in pre-packaged form," Abigail explained.

"Freeze-dried," Emma said proudly.

"What will I need True Brew for?" I asked.

"You never know," they chimed in unison

That sounded suspicious. "Did you see something *else* on your witches' TV?"

"Oh, pish-posh." Abigail smiled. "Just remember...what was that surfing phrase, Emma?"

"Surf's up!" Emma enthused.

Abigail nodded. "Surf's up, dear!"

The day dragged on.

Just as the witches had predicted, I found my violin in the pantry of the school kitchen. I tucked it into my locker, wondering what awful things Chelsea had planned for today's contest.

Tick-tock. Lip-synch. Tick-tock. Lip-synch. I was nervous about dashing onto the stage in my

109

tropical clothes. In the sixth grade, there's a thin line between acting wild and looking downright goofy.

At last, the final bell rang, and students crowded into the halls. Most of the kids headed for the auditorium, hoping to snag the best seats in the audience. I headed for the gym, where the competitors were supposed to assemble.

"You can use the locker rooms to change into your costumes," Mrs. Worst announced, her voice raised above the noise. "But please keep track of all your personal belongings..."

None of the faces in the gym looked familiar as I ducked into the girls' locker room to change. I had just pulled off my sweater when the iciest breath I'd ever felt chilled my neck. Whipping around, I stared into Chelsea's cold eyes.

"You're going to flop," she hissed. "You're going to ruin Kristy's chance to win."

"Thanks for the vote of confidence." I turned away, trying to ignore her.

"Lucky, lucky me," she sang. "With you as the competition, it'll be easier for me to win."

I rolled my eyes. The girl never let up!

Back in the gym, Kristy, Todd, and the rest of our group were in a nervous huddle.

Todd looked up as I came near. "I brought a prop for us."

I followed him to side of the bleachers. A rainbow-striped surfboard was propped against the wall. "Where did you get that?" I asked.

"Before we moved to Lake Trawley, we lived in Santa Monica. I used to surf."

I stared at him. Todd...a surfer dude?

The other kids were all psyched about the surfboard. "We'll use it to carry Kristy onstage," Todd suggested, and the group loved it.

Todd had become an instant hero.

"Here," Kristy said, tossing me a plastic lei to wear around my neck. She'd brought one for everyone in the group. "No matter what happens," she coached us, "just remember to have *fun*."

"Line up!" Mrs. Worst's voice boomed. "All groups should be ready to go!"

Showtime! We were ushered down the hall to one of the rooms behind the auditorium.

"First up, Chelsea Stephens in 'Wild Thing,'" Mrs. Worst announced.

"Now this I gotta see," said Todd.

We stood backstage, watching from the wings. The music started, and Chelsea slithered onto the stage. She was wearing a green sequined dress, and her every movement sparkled.

"She does look like a snake," Kristy said. "I mean, it's a good dance for her."

"The audience likes it," I said, a little bit envious. I didn't like Chelsea, but she could really move. And she *did* look like a snake.

Showered with cheers, she strode offstage. "Beat that," she hissed in my ear as she passed.

Burned, I vowed to do better. I was going to dance and lip-synch as if my life depended on it. It was now or never, time to go for the glory.

Todd and I lifted the surfboard, and one of the other girls helped Kristy climb aboard. She was perched on top when the music started with a twang of guitars.

We marched onto the stage, and the crowd roared in approval. In that moment, I forgot about being afraid. I forgot about everything except being onstage with my friends and giving it my all.

As we mouthed the song, Todd and I lowered the surfboard. Kristy jumped off and danced around us, with the other girls following her. By the time we all formed a line, the kids in the audience were on their feet. They waved their arms, chanting along.

"'Surfin' U.S.A.,'" the crowd sang.

As soon as the last note sounded, we ran off the stage. The sounds of cheers rang in our ears.

"They loved us!" Kristy said in awe.

"Yes!" I couldn't stop grinning.

Todd raised his arms. "We were dy-no-mite!"

"Cowabunga, dudes!" one of the girls shouted.

Laughing and hugging, we headed back to the dressing room. As we squeezed backstage, I saw a flash of blue out of the corner of my eye. The bright blue of *my* knapsack. Someone was swiping it!

Without a word, I ran after the culprit. When she darted behind a panel of curtains, I knew exactly who it was. That glittering green costume could only belong to one girl.

"Put that down, Chelsea!" I demanded when I caught her behind the back curtain, digging through my stuff.

"You're a witch, and I'm going to prove it!"

"You're just upset because I did a lip-synch with Kristy. I think you're jealous."

"*Jealous*!" she shrieked. "Don't make me laugh." She yanked my bag, and everything spilled onto the floor, including the packet of True Brew crystals. "What's this?" She snatched up the packet.

"Nothing." I couldn't quite hide my worry.

"Let me see..." She opened the packet. "What *is* this stuff? Looks like rock candy." She reached into the bag and took out two crystals. They twinkled like gems in the palm of her hand.

But before Chelsea could study the granules,

it happened. The crystals *melted* into her skin.

Poof!

Instantly her flesh turned leathery and dark. Her eyes bugged out. And her arms and legs melted into the rest of her body.

I stumbled backward, a yelp caught in my throat. Before my eyes she turned into a writhing green snake, rising up in a coil.

"Black mamba!" I cried, recognizing the snake from the Nightingales' book.

Hissss! Chelsea bared her curved yellow fangs. She slithered forward, and I remembered the book's description of the black mamba—deadly poisonous.

16

Black Mamba!

I tried to scream, but no sound came out. Paralyzed with fear, I watched the black mamba rear its head back, ready to strike!

"N-n-no!" I choked out. Scrambling back, I slipped and fell.

The snake came slithering after me, hatred gleaming in its eyes. Chelsea was ready to attack when footsteps pounded behind me.

"Jennifer?" Todd called from the other side of the curtain.

"Over here!" I hobbled backward on my rear end.

Chelsea had frozen at the sound of Todd's voice. Her snake head twitched when the curtain moved. One look at Todd, and she darted off toward the backdrop at the rear of the stage.

"What's going on?" Todd stared after the flash of green, then extended a hand to help me up.

"It's Chelsea," I said. "She took some of the

True Brew and turned into a snake—a black mamba. We've got to stop her before she gets away." As I spoke, I gathered my books and the packet of crystals and stuffed them back into the knapsack.

As we ran toward the backdrop, Todd began to digest the whole situation. "Wait a minute. How did Chelsea get the True Brew? And if she's a black mamba, how come she's green?"

"She's an *immature* black mamba. And she got the brew in freeze-dried form," I told him as we ducked behind the backdrop and crossed the stage. "The witches gave me a packet for good luck, and Chelsea took it out of my knapsack."

The song "Achy Breaky Heart" was being pumped through the auditorium, and I knew another act was onstage. If Chelsea slithered out and ruined someone's lip-synch, she deserved to be squashed!

We skidded to a halt at the end of the wing, where furniture and props were stacked high.

"Oh, great," Todd said, taking in the jumble of sofas, chairs, tables, and fake walls. "This is like playing hide-and-seek in a jungle."

I poked around a few chair cushions, then got down on the floor to look under things.

"One more question," he said. "Aren't black mambas poisonous?"

Hissss!

Before I could answer, Chelsea uncoiled from the wooden leg of a chair and her head darted toward me. I jumped back and fell into one of the prop chairs. The snake reared her head back, preparing to strike.

"Gotcha!" Todd's fingers closed around her neck. He snatched her into the air just in the nick of time.

"That's the second time she almost nailed me," I said, scrambling to my feet and brushing off my shorts.

Gripping her below the base of the skull, Todd lifted Chelsea the snake in the air. His nose wrinkled as he frowned at her. "Chelsea's always been quick to attack. But she won't be able to strike while I'm holding her like this."

I felt a rush of relief. Good thing Todd had spent some time being a science nerd. "But you can't hold her forever," I pointed out.

He nodded. "Got any True Brew crystals left?"

"Right here." I opened my knapsack.

"Maybe we should leave her as a snake," Todd said. "We could let her loose in the woods, where she couldn't bother anyone."

"Don't tempt me," I said, staring at the writhing snake. Then that annoying little voice in my head started up again.

"Trust your heart."

"But I can't do it," I decided with a sigh. "I've got to turn her back into an obnoxious girl."

"Can we at least keep her in a cage in the science lab for a few weeks?" Todd said hopefully. "Think of the possibilities!"

I shook my head.

"Too bad," Todd said. "Think she'll learn anything from her True Brew experience?"

"I doubt it." But in a way, Chelsea's transformation had opened my eyes.

I realized that I could use my witchcraft—including spells and brews—any way *I* wanted to. I could learn to control it. It wasn't so scary when I realized that the power wasn't some weird thing floating through the universe. It came from *me*.

"I hope this works," I said, as I picked the blue crystals out of the packet. I looked at Todd. "Ready?" I asked.

He nodded. "Ready as I'll ever be."

17

That Darn Voice

Chelsea's fangs were wet with poison as I dropped the crystals into her mouth.

Poof!

As the mist cleared, I could see Todd tangled up with Chelsea. He was holding her by the hair.

"Eeeewwww!" she squealed. "That's the most disgusting thing that's ever happened to me."

"Me, too." Todd released her and wiped his hands on his shorts.

Smoothing back her hair, Chelsea looked past Todd to where I was standing. "The witch! I should have known. What did you do to me?"

"You did it to yourself," I said. "That's what happens to girls who steal violins and swipe knapsacks."

"How did you—?" Chelsea's eyes flickered nervously from me to Todd. "The violin thing was just a joke. I mean, you're not going to tell anyone. Are you?"

"Not if you keep your nose in your own business—and your own things."

"Some people just can't take a joke," she snapped.

As usual, I couldn't think of a clever comeback. But I stood my ground. I folded my arms and stared at her until she backed away.

Todd was the one who had the last laugh. "Hey, black mamba," he called after her, "how does it feel when the joke's on you?"

"This is it, Jen!" Kristy grabbed my arm. We looked toward Mrs. Worst, who was ready to announce the contest winners. Kids crowded in around us as we waited for the verdict.

"Hey, girls," Todd told everyone, "no matter what happens, we did a great job."

Mrs. Worst called out, "Third place goes to Zoe Winters, Rosie Suarez, and Mae Wong—the Elvisettes—for 'Jailhouse Rock.'"

The crowd clapped.

"Coming in second is John Rizzo for 'Achy Breaky Heart.'"

More applause.

"And first place goes to the 'Surfin' U.S.A.' gang, that's Kristy Geist—"

The rest was drowned out by the cheers that exploded through the auditorium. I barely noticed Chelsea slinking away as we ran onto the stage for a last bow. At last, I was a winner.

"But, Jennifer, didn't you always know you'd win in the end?"

That darn voice...

When our car pulled into the driveway that night, the Nightingales were out watering their flowers. They glided over to greet us.

"How was the contest?" Emma asked.

"We won," I said, even though I was sure she already knew.

"Todd wowed the audience with a real surfboard," Mom offered.

"No big deal." Todd shrugged. "It was fun."

Abigail's eyes flashed behind her spectacles. "If it's not too much trouble, we have some boxes that need to be moved," she said.

"We'll do it," Todd and I offered.

As soon as we reached their front door, Emma turned to us and winked. "Now, tell us *everything*."

"Chelsea turned into a black mamba," I said.

"I wanted to keep her in the snake cage inside the science lab," Todd added, "but Jennifer wouldn't let me."

"Oh, Jennifer, you would have been a fine apprentice," Abigail said. "Can you stay for tea?"

"Nothing fancy, mind you," Emma warned. "All our best china is packed."

As she spoke, the door swung open, revealing dozens of cartons packed along the wall of the living room. "What's going on?" Todd asked.

"Why, we have to move," Abigail explained. "We need to find an apprentice before our powers are gone."

"And before we've completely fizzled," Emma added.

"I want to talk to you about that," I said. "If it's not too late, I've changed my mind. I'd love to be your student."

"Really?" Todd's eyes were wide with excitement. "That's great! Better than scouts. Better than the science club. You are so lucky!"

"Oh, we don't want you to feel pressured, dear," Emma said.

"Come on." I smiled at them. "You must have known that Chelsea would go for the True Brew. That I would see that the power was nothing to fear."

"Did we know that?" Emma looked at her sister.

"Land o' mercy!" Abigail exclaimed. "How could we not know that? We're slipping, Emma."

"Perhaps our radar is rusting," Emma said.

"Oh, but such wonderful news!" Abigail exclaimed. "We must get started immediately."

"Right away," Emma agreed.

The sisters turned toward the stack of boxes, then glanced at each other expectantly.

"Will you, or shall I?" Abigail asked.

"I did the packing," Emma said. "It's your turn, Abigail."

"Oh, all right." Abigail closed her eyes and sighed. *"A place for this, a place for that. Everything should be neat and pat."*

In a flash the room around us changed. The boxes and cartons disappeared. And the parlor was the same as always, with crazy clocks, clawfoot furniture, and one empty birdcage.

"That's much better," Emma said with a sigh.

The cuckoo bird popped out of the grandfather clock and cried, "Trouble, trouble, trouble!"

"What kind of trouble?" I asked.

"Dreadful trouble," Emma said. "There's a young girl who needs our help. Take a look..." She pointed to the painting above the mantel, and suddenly the surface of the canvas went fuzzy.

Images of trees flashed onto the painting. It was like a big-screen TV!

"Cool!" Todd gasped.

Adjusting my glasses, I watched as trees took shape. Walking in the woods was a girl with straight blond hair. Her thoughtful face was familiar. "I think I've met her," I said. It was the girl who'd lent me her violin.

"Her name is Susan," Abigail explained. "And she's in such a pickle. Her mother just lost her job, and her father is sick."

"Such a sweet girl," Emma said sadly, then turned to me. "Are you ready to begin your training?"

I grinned. This was going to be a cinch. "When do I start?"

I mean, what's a witch for, anyway?

Don't miss the next book in the
Shadow Zone series:
**REVENGE OF THE
COMPUTER PHANTOMS**

As I watched, a glowing mist rose from the computer. It was smoking...sort of. My heart began to pound. Was there a fire? Had the *Phantom Quest* program blown the whole system?

A shimmering cloud surrounded the screen.

Then the smoke swirled and formed the face of the gladiator I'd chosen for level four of the game—Thor. From the cloud came curly blond hair, icy blue eyes, and a square jaw that was fixed in a permanent sneer.

I was hallucinating. That was the only explanation.

But Thor was looking more solid with each hammering beat of my heart. His muscular arms formed from the mist. With a grunt, he used them to pull himself right out of the monitor.

He was real...and he was coming after me!